He glanced over at her just as she looked at him.

Jodie wore her hair loose today, and it flowed over her narrow shoulders like melted chocolate. She gave him a wry smile, and for a moment he saw Keith McCauley looking back at him.

"You look just like your father," he said.

You're up on a mountain with a girl you're growing attracted to and that's what you come up with?

He gave himself a mental forehead smack.

"Thanks. I think," she said, pushing her hair away from her face.

Unbidden came the memory of the moment in the corral the other day. Part of him wanted to give in to the attraction he knew was growing between them, but that would be foolish. She was leaving, and in spite of that, she wasn't the right person for him.

Or so you keep saying.

He tried to banish the voice. Tried to be the practical guy he had always strived to be. He didn't want to end up on the wrong side of a broken heart again.

Carolyne Aarsen and her husband, Richard, live on a small ranch in northern Alberta, where they have raised four children and numerous foster children and are still raising cattle. Carolyne crafts her stories in an office with a large west-facing window, through which she can watch the changing seasons while struggling to make her words obey. Visit her website at carolyneaarsen.com.

Books by Carolyne Aarsen

Love Inspired

Big Sky Cowboys

Wrangling the Cowboy's Heart

Lone Star Cowboy League

A Family for the Soldier

Refuge Ranch

Her Cowboy Hero
Reunited with the Cowboy

Hearts of Hartley Creek

A Father's Promise
Unexpected Father
A Father in the Making

Home to Hartley Creek

The Rancher's Return
Daddy Lessons
Healing the Doctor's Heart
Homecoming Reunion
Catching Her Heart

Visit the Author Profile page at Harlequin.com for more titles.

Wrangling the Cowboy's Heart

Carolyne Aarsen

Recycling programs
for this product may
not exist in your area.

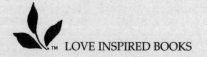 LOVE INSPIRED BOOKS

ISBN-13: 978-0-373-71941-9

Wrangling the Cowboy's Heart

www.Harlequin.com

Printed in U.S.A.

You are my hiding place;
You will protect me from trouble
and surround me with songs of deliverance.
—*Psalms* 32:7

To Linda Ford, who helped me
every step of the way with this book.
Could not have done it without you, girlfriend!
And to Melissa, my editor, who helped
give this story shape and substance.

Both of you are proof that books
are never written in solitude and that
good partnerships make for good stories.

Chapter One

Seriously? Two speeders in half an hour? Was there some unknown crisis people were outrunning?

Deputy Finn Hicks was not in the mood to deal with this. In two hours he was supposed to be delivering the eulogy at his old friend and mentor's funeral. He had one more call, then he hoped to head home, shower and get to the church on time.

But he couldn't let this go. The little blue car blew past him at least twenty miles per hour faster than the posted speed.

Finn pulled in a deep sigh, flicked on the flashers of his cruiser, spun it around and stepped on the gas to catch up with the vehicle speeding toward town. This shouldn't take long if the driver cooperated.

Out-of-state license plates. Broken rear taillight, and it wasn't stopping.

He beeped the siren to get the driver's attention and then, finally, the car slowed and pulled over onto the shoulder.

Finn did a rapid run-through of the plates and his heart turned over in his chest.

Registered to one Jodie McCauley, twenty-seven years old. Female. Resident of Kansas. Onetime girl-friend of one Finn Hicks. If you could call one summer of romance being a girlfriend.

Jodie had no doubt returned to Saddlebank, Montana, for her father's funeral. The same funeral he hoped to attend once his shift was done.

All he had heard lately of Jodie's life had come from his friend Keith. Finn knew Jodie worked as a waitress during the day and played piano in bars at night.

Such a waste of her talent, he had often thought. Jodie had been set to audition for a prestigious music school in Maryland the summer they had dated, ten years ago.

She was also supposed to have gone on another date with him. A date he thought would move things from casual to serious.

She had ditched both appointments and never told him why. The rest of the summer she'd avoided him and hung out with a bad crowd. After that he'd never seen her again.

Until now.

The window rolled down as he came near. Jodie looked up at him through large, dark sunglasses, her mouth pert as always. Thick brown hair flowed over her shoulders, and in her bright red dress and gauzy purple scarf, she looked more as though she was on her way to a party than a funeral.

"Driver's license, insurance and registration, please," he stated, sounding more brusque than he liked.

A reaction to her effect on him.

"Sure thing," she said, handing the papers to him. "Can I ask why you stopped me?"

Her voice was formal, her mouth unsmiling. She didn't seem to recognize him, but then he was wearing sunglasses himself.

"You were speeding, ma'am."

"I understood that the speed limit didn't change for another mile," Jodie said.

"The boundary changed a couple of years ago."

"Has Mayor Milton been digging into the town of Saddlebank's tax coffers again that they need to be replenished with speeding tickets?" she joked, her left elbow resting on the open window, her attitude bordering on cocky.

Still the same boundary-pushing girl he remembered.

"I need your driver's license, Jodie. I mean, ma'am."

Her name slipped out. Most unprofessional of him.

She frowned, then took off her sunglasses.

Eyes blue as a mountain lake and fringed with sooty eyelashes stared up at him, enhanced by dark eyebrows. Her fine features were like porcelain, and combined with her thick, brown hair, it was enough to take his breath away.

Then Jodie glanced down at his chest and he saw the moment she recognized him. Her cocky smile faded away and for a moment, her lashes lowered over her eyes. Her shoulders lifted slowly, as if she was drawing in a calming breath.

"Hey, Finn. Or should I say Sheriff Hicks?" Her voice held a faintly taunting note, which bothered him more than he cared to admit.

"It's deputy. Sheriff Donnelly is still around," he said, unable to stop the confused flow of memories as he thought of her father sitting by himself at the dining room table of the ranch he owned, lamenting the fact that his three daughters never came to visit anymore. Keith McCauley had been a good friend and mentor to Finn, helping him through a rough time in his life after his father died when Finn was fifteen. Finn's mother had retreated into herself after that, and then Finn had come home from school one bitterly cold March day to find out her gone. She had left a note on the table telling him she needed to focus on her musical career. That she would be back. She just wasn't sure when.

Worried about his mother, Finn had called Keith, who'd been a deputy at the time. Keith had come and driven him to his house. The next day he'd brought him over to the Moore family, who had taken him in. Finn's mother had come home four months later, and he'd moved back in with her. But a week later she'd left again.

Though she'd popped in and out of his life after that, he'd stayed with the Moores until he could move out on his own.

Keith had encouraged him and helped him through that difficult time. It had been Keith who'd introduced him to his fiancée, Denise. Keith who had encouraged him to date her after Keith had met her at the hospital in Bozeman.

"Hate to rush the long arm of the law," Jodie said, her voice holding a surprisingly tight note, "but am I getting a ticket or...?"

Finn mentally shook off the sad memories. "In honor of your father, a man I admired, I'll let you off today," he said, meeting her gaze. "He was a good man."

She looked up at him, her blue eyes flat now. Expressionless. "I'm sure he was good to you."

Her cryptic comment confused him, but he guessed

her emotions were volatile on a day like today, so he let it go. He had heard from Keith that his three daughters had planned to visit him after his cancer diagnosis. But before that happened Keith had been killed when his truck rolled upside down.

Finn stood aside as Jodie rolled up the window, started the car.

He half expected her to peel off, tires spinning, but she slowly pulled away, keeping to the speed limit this time.

Her car topped the rise, the heat shimmering up from the pavement, distorting it, and then it dropped into the valley, disappearing from view.

Now he had to finish his shift, clean up and try to get to the funeral on time. But as he drove to his last call of the day, all his thoughts were of those blue, blue eyes.

Jodie clutched the single rose she held, staring at the casket bearing the remains of her father as the pastor read from the Bible. With her other arm she clung to her sister Lauren as a flock of ravens whistled overhead. The birds were a funereal black against the blue Montana sky that stretched from one mountain range to the other, cradling the basin the town of Saddlebank nestled in.

She took in a deep breath, slowing her still-racing heart, memories as raucous as the birds above them swirling through her mind. The service in the church had been mercifully brief and surprisingly difficult. Jodie's own emotions were so mixed as she listened to the pastor talking about her father's life. She wondered if they knew the same person.

Do not speak ill of the dead.

Her grandmother's words resounded in Jodie's mind. Her dear grandmother, who had also passed on, like Jodie's mother had. So many losses, she thought.

Only half her attention was on the casket and the pastor. The other half was on the man who stood toward the back of the sparse crowd assembled around the grave.

He was taller than the last time she'd seen him. Which wasn't a memory she enjoyed pulling out.

That summer had been both wonderful and awful. She'd dated Finn, and lost her chance at her audition for the music conservatory.

After her parents' divorce and their subsequent move to Knoxville with their mom, she and her sisters had spent their summers in Saddlebank with their father. He'd never approved of her seeing Finn. Keith McCauley thought Finn Hicks was too good for her.

But at the beginning of that summer Jodie had felt her life was coming to a good place. She was falling in love with a wonderful guy. Which had scared her, and led her to do something very stupid.

She was still dealing with the repercussions of that decision and her father's reaction to this day. After that summer, she'd never seen Finn again.

Until a couple hours ago.

Seeing Finn in the same uniform her father always wore, a uniform that evoked too many bad memories, was a shock, and yet not a surprise. Finn had always been a solid, salt-of-the-earth guy. Which was what had attracted her to him initially.

She wondered what he would think of her now, working as a waitress during the day, playing piano in bars at night.

Jodie sneaked another glance at Finn, dismayed to

catch him returning her gaze. But he looked quickly away, his hazel eyes now focused on Keith's coffin. Finn had grown from an appealing teen into a handsome man, his strong features, square chin and broad shoulders granting him an authority that seemed ingrained. His dark brown hair, worn longer than her father's regulation haircut, curled just enough to soften his face.

She shouldn't have been surprised that Finn had followed in her father's footsteps. The eulogy Finn had delivered a few moments ago was lavish in his praise of a man he'd said had been a mentor to him. A shining example of Christian love in quiet action.

It had been a difficult funeral, Jodie thought, clenching and unclenching her right hand. Leaning on her sister as she so often did.

Lauren wore a sensible black dress, a stark and suitable contrast to her own bright red one. Jodie had refused to wear black, reasoning that with her dark hair she'd look washed out, but now she felt a touch of regret at her choice. She looked as though she didn't care, when, in fact, her emotions concerning her dad were complex and confusing.

For better or for worse, he was still her father, and now he was gone.

Her older sister stared at the coffin, her pale face framed by her long blond hair, her blue eyes blinking, her narrow shoulders hunched protectively. She pressed Jodie's arm to her side.

Jodie wondered if she, too, thought of their missing sister, Lauren's twin. When they had contacted Erin to make the arrangements, all Lauren or Jodie had got in reply were terse text messages stating she couldn't come. Nothing else.

At a signal from the pastor, Lauren laid her rose on the casket. Jodie did the same, followed by Aunt Laura, their father's sister. Their aunt was short and plump, her graying hair cut in a shoulder-length bob. She wore a simple gray blazer, slacks and sensible shoes, as befitting the funeral of her brother. She placed her rose on the coffin, then stepped aside to let Monty Bannister, a tall, heavyset man who was their father's distant cousin, and his wife, Ellen, who barely made it to Monty's shoulder, do the same.

"In the name of the Father, Son and the Holy Spirit, we commend the body of our brother Keith McCauley to the ground," Pastor Dykstra said, his voice tugged away on the breeze swirling around the graveyard. "And we cling to the promise of the resurrection of the dead. The hope of our eternal life."

Jodie said a quiet amen, a shiver traveling down her spine at the thought of eternal life. Facing God with the mess that had been her life the past ten years. That was one of the reasons she'd avoided God lately.

The casket slowly descended into the ground, and with each inch Jodie felt the complicated bonds tethering her to her father loosen. It had been years since she'd last seen him. Years since that horrible fight that had changed her life, broken the connection between her and Finn and sent her running away from him and everything he represented.

She'd called her father a few times a year. Each time she'd been on the receiving end of a litany of complaints and grumblings, and guilt piled on her for not coming to see him.

Then he had been diagnosed with cancer. But only

weeks before she and her sisters had arranged to visit, their father was killed in a single-vehicle accident.

"The family would like to invite everyone to meet in the church hall for some lunch," Pastor Dykstra announced, ending the funeral service.

People started drifting away and Jodie took a deep breath, knowing what lay ahead. Well-wishers and sympathy and a headache that increased with each passing moment. She caught a glimpse of Finn walking to another part of the graveyard, then stopping by a stone.

Jodie wondered if it was his father's grave, remembering that his dad had died when Finn was only fourteen.

Finn's smile was melancholy as he looked down, then ran his fingers over the stone, as if trying to connect with whoever was buried there. His sorrow caught at her heart. She doubted she would ever look at her father's grave with the same love that seemed to shine in Finn's eyes.

"I'm so sorry for your loss," Pastor Dykstra said as he shook Lauren's hand, resting his other on Jodie's shoulder. Jodie focused her attention back on the man with another surge of remorse. "Your father talked often of you girls."

Pastor Dykstra shook Jodie's hand, his kindly eyes holding hers. "I pray you will let God comfort you at this time."

She nodded, giving him a smile. He squeezed her hand again, then walked away from the grave toward the church.

Monty Bannister also shook Jodie's, then Lauren's hand. "I hope that you'll be able to remember some of the good times you had with your father," he said, giving them both a winsome smile. "And that you feel God's presence in your lives."

Jodie wasn't sure how to respond to that. She hadn't spent a lot of time with God lately and doubted that He cared to spend much time with her. Nor was she so sure which memories of her father she would be remembering. When she and her sisters had come to visit, it was as if he hadn't known what to do with his daughters other than make them work. Each summer had been fraught with the tension of living with a man who, as sheriff of Saddlebank County, saw life in black-and-white. No shades of gray. A man who for some reason was especially hard on Jodie.

So she simply murmured her thanks. She was quite certain that even if Monty knew exactly what her father was like, he would have said the same thing.

"You girls make sure you call us if you need anything," Ellen told them, clinging to both their hands, her smile warm.

"Thank you," Jodie and Lauren said at the same time.

Jodie had only vague remembrances of Monty, Ellen and their three children, Keira, Heather and Lee. Keith had taken them only a few times to Refuge Ranch, the Bannister spread. Because Lauren and Erin were older, they'd hung out with Keira and Heather, leaving Jodie to play with either the cats in the barn or the horses.

"How are you girls holding out?" Aunt Laura slipped an arm around Lauren, giving Jodie a quick smile.

"This is harder than I thought it would be," Lauren said, wiping her eyes. "I feel so bad that we didn't take the time to see him before he died."

"Oh, honey, you meant to," their aunt assured her. "I know you were making plans. He was excited at the thought of seeing you both. I'm sure you have good and bad memories, and like cousin Monty said, I hope you can find some of the good ones," she continued.

"Thanks, Aunt Laura," Jodie said, giving her a hug. "It's so good to see you again."

"We'll have to make sure to get together while you girls are still here. Knowing you, Jodie, you'll be gone with the first puff of wind sifting through the valley." Aunt Laura raised her finely plucked eyebrows. "I'll give you girls a moment while I make certain the caterer has taken care of the lunch."

As their aunt marched off to do her duty, Lauren took a deep breath, blinking back tears, and pulled a tissue out of the pocket of her dress. "I can't believe I feel this way," she sniffed. "I didn't think I'd be so weepy."

"Part of it might be because Erin's not here," Jodie said, tucking her arm in her sister's. "You two always had a special bond."

A bond that Jodie, at times, envied. Her twin sisters always seemed so self-sufficient, and though they included Jodie in many of their antics and adventures, she often felt like an outsider to their relationship.

"Why wouldn't she come?" Lauren asked, the pain she felt evident in her voice.

"Obviously something's happening in her life and she needs to deal with it." That was all Jodie could say.

Her sister gave her a wan smile. "How are you doing? Today can't be easy for you, either."

Though Lauren had often witnessed Jodie and her father's altercations, she had never been subject to his intense anger, as Jodie had been whenever she messed up. It didn't help that the two of them had the same quick temper.

Jodie had spent way more hours in "time out" than her sisters. It had only increased her rebelliousness, finally ending with her stopping her visits to the ranch.

"It's hard," she said now, emotions braiding through her memories as she tried to find the good ones that the pastor suggested she look for.

Lord, forgive me, she thought. *I can't think of many.*

Chapter Two

Keith's funeral service was harder to deal with than Finn had expected it would be.

Though Finn came to church every Sunday, the atmosphere there today and at the graveyard afterward reminded him of his fiancée's funeral four years ago. Except then the church had been packed and the people surrounding the grave spilled over into the parking lot—all grieving with Finn over a life taken so young.

As he'd followed Denise's casket out of the church that sad day, Finn thought he would never love anyone again, never find anyone as sweet and caring as Denise.

And he hadn't, though lately a loneliness had begun to affect him. Loneliness and a growing dissatisfaction with his life.

It didn't help that, after popping erratically in and out of his life over the past thirteen years, his mother had contacted him again a couple weeks ago. After Denise had died, the only thing he'd got from his mom had been a card with the words *I'm sorry* scrawled inside. He was thankful he'd had the support of the Moore family and Keith during that time.

Finn shook off the heavy emotions as he looked down at the memorial card the funeral director had handed him when he came into the church. Keith's stern face with his distinctive handlebar mustache stared back at him, his eyes distant. The picture was an older one Finn had taken when he and Keith had spent more time together. Was it his imagination or did he see the loneliness the man had endured over the years?

Remorse washed over Finn again as he thought of how he had neglected him recently.

At one time, Finn had spent all his extra hours at Keith's ranch, helping him with his horses while he learned farrier work. After Finn's own father died and his mother had abandoned him, Keith had been like a father to him.

But the past few years Keith had pulled away. Hadn't returned Finn's calls, wouldn't come to church. Finn had been grieving the loss of Denise, lost in his own sorrow.

He smoothed his hand over his tie, blinked back the fatigue that pulled at him after a long shift and forced a sympathetic smile to his face as the line moved on.

Lauren, one of the twins, was the first person he saw, her face drawn, her long blond hair and dark dress a sharp contrast to her younger sister's dark hair and red dress. The only similarity was the narrowness of their features. Like their mother, Finn thought, remembering a family photo he had seen the first time he'd visited the ranch.

Finn was surprised that Erin, Lauren's twin sister, was absent. Of all the girls she seemed to love being at the ranch every summer the most.

"I'm sorry for your loss," Finn said to Lauren when he stepped up to her.

"Thanks for coming, Finn. My father thought a lot of you." She gave him a weary smile. "I'm sure you'll miss him."

"I will. He was good to me."

He moved on to Jodie, surprised once more at how easily his own memories and emotions returned.

"Hello again, Jodie. Long time."

"That it is." She glanced up at him, and once again he felt the impact of her unsettling gaze, the contrast of her almost black hair and her intensely blue eyes. She had been pretty when she was younger. Now she was stunning, and as he shook her hand, the loneliness that lingered since Denise's death made him hold it longer than was proper.

"Glad you could make the funeral on time," he said.

Her mouth curved in a faint smile and the ghost of a dimple appeared in one cheek.

"All thanks to you," she said. "I appreciate getting out of the ticket."

He frowned, glancing around. "Don't say that too loud. I have a reputation to uphold."

Jodie laughed, catching the attention of a few people. "Well, according to Shakespeare, reputation is a burden, got without merit and lost without deserving…or something like that."

That made Finn smile. "Did you remember that or did you make that up?"

"Google it and find out."

He held her eyes a moment, surprised at how easy it was to fall back into the give-and-take that had attracted him the first time he talked to her. Then he caught himself. He was at a funeral, and this was Jodie. A girl more like his absent mother than his beloved fiancée. How could he forget that?

"I also want to give you condolences from Sheriff Donnelly," Finn continued, finally pulling his hand away. "He would have come but he was busy, so he asked me to represent him, as well. Donnelly always said your father was a good sheriff. Tough, but fair."

Jodie's smiled faded. "Yes. That was Dad. Keeping the world safe for carbon-based life forms."

Finn wanted to smile at her quip, which was the same thing Keith McCauley had always said, but the bitterness in her voice quenched that. He didn't know what to make of it.

"Anyway, I'm sure you and your sisters will have lots to deal with in the next few days," he continued. "Will you be staying at the Rocking M, I mean your father's ranch?"

"I will be for a couple of days. Hopefully we can get everything sorted out by then and I'll be on my way," Jodie said. She shifted her weight, as if moving away from him, and Finn got the hint. She hadn't changed, he told himself. Jodie McCauley, on the move.

Ever since he'd watched her drive away a few hours ago, he'd found himself thinking of their past, of how Jodie had meant something to him.

When he was eighteen, it had taken him weeks to work up enough courage to ask out the daughter of his mentor, the sheriff.

He finally had and to his surprise she had accepted. They'd had a good time. He'd thought they'd connected. But she'd always insisted on meeting in Mercy, a small town thirty miles down the valley. Finn hadn't liked sneaking around, but she'd been insistent.

On their dates they would talk about their plans for the future—he wanted to start his own ranch, she wanted to play piano professionally. They would share jokes, laugh and make other plans to meet.

He'd thought things were getting serious, but then she'd stood him up one night.

The next day he'd been shocked to see her in town. She was supposed to have been leaving for Maryland that morning for an audition for the Peabody Institute, a music conservatory. Instead, she'd been hanging on the arm of Jaden Woytuk, local bad boy, laughing about the bandage on her hand that kept slipping off.

Later Finn had found out she'd gone to a party at Jaden's place the night of their date. She'd stood him up to hang out with that rough crowd.

The rest of the summer Jodie's reputation as a wild girl just got worse. And when she'd left to go home to Knoxville, that was the last he'd seen of her.

Until today.

She stood by her sister now, talking with Monty and Ellen, from Refuge Ranch. Her smile softened her features and then, to his surprise, she glanced his way. Their eyes met and he felt again that old quiver of attraction.

"Finn Hicks. I need to talk to you."

Finn dragged his attention away from Jodie to the man standing in front of him, a mug of coffee in one hand, a chocolate brownie in the other. Vic Moore was easily as tall as Finn, but blond where he was dark, his shoulders broader. And his face was the kind that Finn knew women found attractive, with slashing eyebrows framing deep-set eyes, full lips and a strong chin. Good thing he was like a brother to Finn or he might not like him as much as he did.

"Hey, Moore." Finn poured himself some coffee, then grabbed a brownie, which would have to do until he could get a decent meal. "What can I do for you?"

"First off, good eulogy."

"Thanks, though it didn't seem to say enough. I'll always be grateful for the support and guidance Keith gave me."

"You had a good relationship with him."

"I did. I'll miss the guy." Finn felt a touch of guilt. The past few years, he and Keith had drifted apart. Finn had gotten busier with his job as sheriff's deputy and his growing business as a farrier and horse trainer.

"Do you have time to come over tomorrow and help me round up the horses I have pastured at Keith's ranch?" Vic asked.

"Donnelly has me on a light schedule this week but I'll figure it out." For Finn, any time spent with horses was a good day.

"Dean and I hoped to do some riding," Vic continued. "My brother needs some distraction, and the physiotherapist cleared him to ride. But I first have to get the horses together. I figured it would be best, now that Keith is gone, to get my horses off the ranch."

"I'll make it work." Because he was still establishing his farrier and training business, Finn tried to fit in any potential job.

Suddenly he heard a burst of laughter, which was odd considering the circumstances, and sought out the source. Jodie stood beside Drake Neubauer, Keith's lawyer, smiling at something he had just said.

"She's even prettier than when she lived here, isn't she?" Vic said.

Finn startled, feeling as if he'd been caught doing something illegal. "What do you mean?"

"Keith's girl. Lauren."

Guess Vic was too busy scoping out the older sister to notice Finn doing the same with Jodie.

"Yeah. She is," he conceded. With her blond hair and blue eyes, Lauren reminded him of Denise, but the comparison ended with the stern lines on her face. Truth to tell, of the three sisters, Jodie had always intrigued him the most. The combination of her smart mouth and her troubled expression when he'd stopped her car today created a disconnect with the Jodie from his past, one that piqued his curiosity. She looked as if life had thrown her some hard curves since she'd left Saddlebank.

"Funny how those girls can be sisters, but each be so different," Vic said, taking another sip of his coffee. "Jodie still seems to have that reckless air."

"She was a pistol," Finn agreed.

"That girl could outdrive, outride most of the guys in the county that last summer she was here. It was just 'cause Donnelly and Keith were buddies that Jodie managed to duck as many charges she did."

Finn's cheeks flushed as he thought of how he had let her off a speeding ticket himself a few hours ago.

He tried to convince himself it was merely common courtesy and had nothing to do with anything Jodie said or did.

And nothing to do with those striking blue eyes and glossy dark hair.

"You gonna ask her out again?" Vic gave him a

nudge with his elbow. "Not too many single girls that good-looking come through Saddlebank. I'm sure she's settled down some since she was younger."

"I doubt I'll be asking," Finn said, remembering too well a girl who'd spent most of that last summer she was here partying, drinking and challenging her father at every opportunity. "I don't think I'm interested."

"Jodie's no Denise, that's for sure," Vic continued. "But she is single. I think you should give her another chance. Maybe this time she won't stand you up."

"You're joking, right?" Finn asked.

"Of course I am. Wouldn't want to mess up your ten-year plan," Vic said, laughing, then sauntered out of the hall without a backward glance.

Finn shook his head at his friend's comment. He had to have a plan, he reminded himself. Changing plans and ditching people was his mother's MO. There was no way he was going to live that kind of life.

As for Jodie, his reaction to her had more to do with her past than her present. He needed to forget it. Move on.

He downed the last of his coffee. He had a few things to do at work before he headed to the Grill and Chill to grab a bite to eat. Then he'd get back to his ranch to work with a horse he was training.

But before he left he allowed himself another glance Jodie's way.

Only to find her looking at him, a peculiar expression on her face.

"So what can we do about this?"

Jodie held up the letter their father's lawyer had just given them, the noise of the Grill and Chill diner a counterpoint to the frustration simmering in her.

After the funeral, she and Lauren had met with Drake Neubauer, their father's lawyer, at his office to go over the will.

For the most part, it was straightforward. He had bequeathed half the cash in his account to the church. The rest was for any unexpected expenses incurred by his death. The ranch, horses, equipment and any remaining assets were to be split equally among the three girls.

But this letter was a complication that seemed typical of their father's need for control.

"Read it again," Lauren said wearily. She leaned back against the booth, dragging her hands over her gaunt cheeks. Jodie guessed the weariness pulling at her sister had as much to do with her humiliation over being left at the altar eighteen months ago as Erin's puzzling and disturbing no-show at the funeral. Their sister's only contact with them the past six months had been brief text messages that communicated nothing more than basic information. Lauren and Jodie were both concerned.

"'I know that I haven't been the best father.'" Jodie stifled a sigh at that particular understatement as she continued reading the letter aloud. "'I know you girls never wanted to leave Knoxville and come to the ranch every summer after your mother died. I know you only came because your grandmother insisted.'" Jodie shook her head after she read that. "I don't know why that bothers me," she said. "It's not as though he wanted us there, either."

"No editorializing," Lauren said with a wave of her hand.

Jodie cleared her throat and continued.

"'But it was your first home. That's why you're getting it when I die. This cancer is gonna kill me one way or the other. And I know you're gonna sell the ranch as soon as you get it. But before you can sell it, I want each of you to spend two months on the ranch. I talked to Drake Neubauer, and he said I should change my will officially, but until I do that, consider this a condition of inheriting the ranch. You girls never appreciated it like I knew you should. So this is what I want you to do before you can sell the place. If you don't want to stay, you lose your part of the inheritance. If none of you want to stay, then I made other plans. Drake will let you know what happens if that's the case. Dad.'"

Jodie clutched the paper, stifling her annoyance. "This is so typical of Dad. Has he ever given us anything without a proviso attached? It seems as if every job or chore he wanted us to do was issued as a nonnegotiable decree."

"You might be reading more into this than meets the eye," Lauren replied, ever the peacemaker. "You and Dad always had a volatile relationship."

Lauren knew only the half of it. When she and Erin turned eighteen, they'd stopped coming to the ranch. Both had gone to college and took on summer jobs, leaving Jodie to spend two more summers alone with their father. They'd fought at every turn, Jodie often on the receiving end of his anger.

She tamped down the memories, as she always did when they threatened.

And how are you going to keep them at bay for two months if you stay?

"I always figured Dad and I never got along because I was the only one who got to see the big fight that changed everything," Jodie said, fingering one edge of the letter.

Jodie had been in the barn loft, playing with kittens, when she'd heard her parents' raised voices below her. She'd come down to see her father yelling at their mother to leave the ranch and take her daughters with her. Jodie, shocked and defensive of her mom, had yelled at him not to talk to her that way. But he'd ignored her, walking away. Her mother and sisters had left the ranch the next day and Jodie had never forgiven him. She was only seven at the time.

"It didn't help that you always egged him on," Lauren continued.

"It also didn't help that he never believed me when I told him I'd just been out with friends, and not partying like he always accused me of."

"Well, you were partying, toward the end."

"Only because I figured I may as well do what he always accused me of, and have fun."

"Was it fun?"

Jodie caught the unspoken reprimand in her sister's tone and looked down at the letter.

It was an echo of the one she'd voiced whenever Jodie had tried to tell her sisters about what had really happened those summers alone on the ranch. They'd often questioned her, citing the steady antagonism between Jodie and her father as the reason. So she'd kept her mouth shut, endured her father's alternating stony silences and spewing anger.

And, increasingly, his physical punishment.

"So what do we do about this?" Jodie said, resting her elbows on the scarred Formica table.

"I'm too busy to take two months away from work," Lauren said, clutching her coffee mug. "Things are too iffy with my job. Would it stand up in court if we don't agree to the terms of the letter? Could we still sell the ranch and get the money?"

"This document was verified by the lawyer..." Jodie let the sentence fade away as she skimmed the letter again. Her father's distinct scrawl covered the page, and below that was a note from Drake Neubauer proving this was indeed Keith McCauley's handwriting and that this was a legal and binding document. "I can see why Dad wanted us to read this after the funeral. I'm sure if I heard it before, I would have had a hard time concentrating on the service."

Not that Finn's presence had made it easier.

"What do you suppose the ranch is worth?" Lauren asked.

"Enough to help us out in our own ventures, I would guess," Jodie said. "Might be something you'd want to look into before you decide you can't do this."

"And you?"

Jodie shrugged. "Money's never been that important to me."

Lauren looked as if she was about to say something more when their waitress brought a bowl of soup and a salad for Lauren, pizza and onion rings for Jodie.

"That is the most unhealthy combination of foods I can imagine," Lauren sniffed as the waitress left.

"It feeds my soul as well as my stomach," Jodie said,

grabbing the bottle of ketchup to douse her onion rings. "Comfort food."

"I guess we could both use some of that." Lauren gave her a rueful smile, then bowed her head.

With a guilty start Jodie realized her sister was praying a silent blessing over her food. Belatedly she followed suit.

Forgive me, Lord, she prayed. *I haven't talked a lot to You lately. I'm sorry. I haven't felt as if I have the right. My life's been a mess, so I guess I could use some help there.* Regret and remorse rose up again as the memories surfaced. But she caught herself in time. The past was done, even though the pain and repercussions lingered.

She finished her prayer with a thank-you for her food.

"So tell me about this music gig you'll be doing?" Lauren asked. "Any future in it?"

Trust her to cut to the chase. Ever the older sister, Lauren had always been after Jodie to find something that gave her a career.

"It's not a huge job and there's no guarantee," Jodie said. "But if it goes well, there's a good chance that the band will open for this new breakout group. We might be touring with them."

"*Might* be."

Jodie waved off Lauren's comment. "Everything in this business is hearsay or odds. Besides, I'll find work waitressing if I need to fill in any gaps."

"And what about your composing? Would you be able to keep doing that?"

"I don't know if I'd have the time," Jodie said, feeling a vague pang. "If this gig doesn't happen, I'll work enough to save up for a trip to Thailand. Maybe write some music there."

"Running again?"

Jodie felt a flare of indignation at the censure in her sister's voice. "It's called traveling. Expanding your horizons. You should try it sometime instead of tying yourself to your job."

"My job gives me security. Something you don't seem to have. Besides, I don't know how you can afford all these trips."

"Simple. No obligations. Nothing pinning me down. Free as a bird." Jodie waved her hand as if underlining her mantra. "Driving an old car and taking in tips help."

"You'll never settle down, living the life you do. You'll never find anyone."

"Don't need anyone. Not after Lane."

"Lane was a mistake. I don't think the two of you were suited to each other."

Though she knew Lauren was right, her sister's comment struck at Jodie's latent insecurities. It had taken her almost a year to get past the anger and pain she felt when her former fiancé had broken up with her.

He had asked for his ring back after he saw a stranger flirting with Jodie while she worked her second job, playing piano at a bar.

Lane had always wanted her to quit that job. He'd felt that, as the son of a US senator, he had a reputation to uphold.

But Jodie knew she had no other marketable skills. She valued her independence and the money she made, so she'd stayed with it. Then one night one of her regular patrons had sat down beside her, put his arm around her and kissed her on the cheek just as Lane had come in. Jodie had denied there was anything going on between them, but Lane had chosen not to believe her and had asked for his ring back.

Two weeks later she'd found out he was dating the daughter of a minister. A much more suitable woman for someone like him.

Jodie hadn't been in a serious relationship since.

"You deserve someone who accepts you for who you are," Lauren continued.

"Doesn't matter." She shrugged off her sister's protests. "Since I haven't found anyone who interests me enough to think of settling down, I prefer to be the one in charge. Be the one walking away."

As soon as the words left her lips, she realized how they might sound to her sister, whose fiancé had walked away from her the morning of their wedding.

"Sorry," she said quietly. "I didn't mean to say that."

"Doesn't matter," Lauren muttered, but Jodie could see from the tightness around her lips that it did. Jodie had been with her sister when she'd gotten the news. Lauren had been just about to put on her wedding dress. Instead, her normally composed sister had kicked it aside, tossed her bouquet down and stormed out of the room, leaving Erin and Jodie to take care of all the details.

"Anyway, I don't want to be tied down."

"Well, with the life you live, you don't have time to give anyone else a chance," Lauren said, lifting her head. "Maybe staying in one place for two months might be just what you need."

Much as Jodie trumpeted her freedom, the idea of being at the ranch held a reluctant allure. The past couple years she'd had a curious yearning, the strange feeling that she'd been missing something. The trips, the traveling, the work—nothing satisfied her as it used to. She couldn't quite put her finger on why.

"And maybe, if you stay in one place, you might have time to spend with Finn again," Lauren continued.

Jodie started. "What are you talking about?"

"I saw how you watched him at the funeral service, and then the reception after," Lauren said, giving her sister a vague smile.

"I was thinking about how he stopped me for speeding."

"Oh, c'mon. He was just doing his job. And look how sweet he is, chatting up the locals over at the other table."

Finn was here? Jodie couldn't resist a glance over her shoulder.

Deputy Hicks stood by a table, talking with a group of older women. He seemed to dominate the space, his back ramrod straight, his white shirt and blue jeans softening his military stance. It shouldn't surprise her that Finn had ended up in law enforcement. The man had made no secret of his admiration for her father.

"A little too 'serve and protect' for my liking. Like Dad. No, thanks," she said, with what she hoped was a dismissive tone.

Then Finn turned around and looked her way. Their eyes met across the distance and his expression altered. In that moment Jodie felt a whisper of the old attraction.

No. Not for you, she told herself. *You and guys equal disaster.* Especially someone like Finn.

She dragged her eyes away, focusing on her onion rings. Then felt Lauren's foot nudging her under the table. "He's coming this way," she hissed. "Fix your lipstick."

Jodie gave her sister the evil eye, hoping she got the message—Not Interested.

"Afternoon, ladies," Finn said, looking from Jodie to Lauren. "I thought I would come by to say hello again. Hope this day wasn't too difficult for you. I know it didn't start off the best."

He caught Jodie's eye and she knew he referred to their interaction this morning. She blushed, thinking of her smart remarks, but brushed the memory aside.

"We'll get through it." She gave him a polite smile.

"I didn't have time to tell you after the funeral, but I wanted to say how thankful I always was for your father's support. He was a good man. He missed you girls a lot. He often spoke about you and how he wished you could visit more often."

Jodie took a moment to respond to that, then felt another nudge from her sister's toe.

"I'm sure he did," she finally replied. "It's been difficult to find time to come."

Her empty words sounded shallow, even to her. She'd managed to find time to go to Asia, India and Paris, but not a trip to Saddlebank? But she wasn't about to apologize for her lack of filial duty.

"I also thought I should let you know that Vic and I will be coming to your place tomorrow. Your dad let Vic pasture a bunch of his horses there, and we want to sort them out of your father's herd. I wanted to give you a heads up in case you're wondering what's going on."

"Thanks for telling us," Lauren said. "Jodie will be staying at the ranch, so if you need anything you can ask her."

Jodie pushed her sister's foot this time, but Lauren smiled, ignoring her.

"I think we'll be okay. And I wish you girls the best," he said, looking from one to the other. "Hope settling the estate won't be too painful and you manage to find some happier memories." Just before he left, his eyes met Jodie's.

And for a heartbeat their gazes locked and she wondered if he was referring to their shared past.

Then he put his hat back on his head and left. The moment was gone.

Jodie grabbed an onion ring and swiped it through the pile of ketchup on her plate, surprised at the emotions churning through her where Finn was concerned.

Lauren leaned forward, her eyes glinting with amusement. "I think he still likes you. I saw how he stared at you now."

"You saw what you wanted to see. I saw a man who thinks we're lousy daughters who didn't visit a man he thought the sun rose and set on."

"He was just making conversation. He still seems interested in you."

"Maybe it was you he was interested in," Jodie countered. "I was the one that stood him up, remember? Besides, he's a deputy now. Not the kind of guy I'd be attracted to. Been there, done that."

"Not all men are like Dad, you know," Lauren said. "And not all men are like Lane. Once upon a time you were attracted to Finn."

Jodie's only answer was to take a bite of her pizza. Her sister was right, but she wasn't about to let someone like Finn into her life again.

He was too much a reminder of all that she had lost. All that her father had taken away. And she couldn't let herself feel that vulnerable again.

Chapter Three

Jodie stepped into the house, déjà vu washing over her as the faintest scent of onions and bacon, her father's favorite foods, wafted past her. Vague evidence that he had been here only a week ago.

Pain clenched her heart. Pain and regret, coupled with a wish that Lauren could have come with her to the Rocking M.

Her sister had had to leave early this morning to catch a plane, so last night they'd stayed in Saddlebank's only motel, then gone their separate ways at dawn.

Jodie toed off her boots and put them on the shelf under the coatrack. She set her suitcase on the old wooden bench, as she and her sisters always did the day they arrived at the ranch. For a fraction of a moment loneliness nudged her at the sight of her lone suitcase. There should be two more.

She paused, listening, but the only sounds in the stillness were the ticking of the grandfather clock in the living room and the hum of the refrigerator in the rear.

Hugging herself, she walked through the house to the kitchen. A breakfast bar bisected the space, separating the cooking area from the rest of the room. She and her sisters had spent a lot of time there, laughing as they created unique meals using the minimal ingredients available to them. Their father had never been big on shopping.

A large room took up the far end of the house, the ceiling soaring two stories high. The dining room table with its five mismatched chairs filled one side, while couches and a couple recliners huddled around the stone fireplace on the far wall, flanked by two large bay windows.

A baby grand piano, covered with a flowered sheet, took up the far corner of the room. Jodie was surprised her dad still had it. It was an older one from her aunt Laura, who used to teach piano.

Jodie's smile faded as she looked toward the closed door of her father's office.

How many times had he pulled her into that room, ordered her to sit in the chair and listen? How many lectures had she endured, with him pounding his fist on the desk, telling her she was a disgrace to his good name? It didn't take much to resurrect his angry voice berating her, the sting of his hand on her cheek.

She spun away from the office, striding toward the living room as if outrunning the hurtful memories. She stopped at the window overlooking the yard. From there she saw the wooden fences of the corrals edging the rolling green pastures. Beyond them stood the mountains, snow still clinging to the peaks even in summer.

During the days of stifling heat in Knoxville, she'd definitely missed the mountains and the open spaces of this ranch. She fingered the curtain, leaning her forehead against the cool glass of the window, the usual daydreams assaulting her. Travel, moving, being in charge of where she went instead of working around other people's plans for her life. She had spent most of her childhood going where others told her to go, being who others told her to be. Now she was stuck here for a couple months, once again, her situation being dictated by her father.

She could leave. She knew that. Forfeit her right to a portion of the ranch. But she also knew the reality of her situation. Any money she got from selling the ranch would be a huge benefit. Touring wouldn't be the financial hardship it usually was.

And what would Dad think of that?

She pushed aside the guilt and mixed feelings that had been her steady companions since her father died, then walked over to the piano and pulled the sheet off, sneezing at the dust cloud she created. Lifting the lid, she propped it open, raised the fallboard covering the keys and sat down at the bench.

She ran a few scales, the notes echoing in the emptiness. Surprisingly, the piano was still reasonably in tune.

Her fingers unerringly found the notes of "Für Elise," one of the first pieces she had ever performed, and its haunting melody filled the silence as memories assailed her.

Sitting at this same piano, her pudgy fingers plinking out notes of the scales as her sisters played outside. Often her time at the piano was punishment for one of her many misdeeds. Between the musical aptitude her grandmother tried to nurture and the many times Jodie got into trouble, she'd spent a lot of time at the keyboard.

But while music had, initially, been a burden, it had

eventually became a release. She took her skills and applied them to writing music, something that she enjoyed.

And now, as she played in her childhood home once again, the music transported her to better times, better memories.

The light from the window fell across the keys and, as she often did when she was playing, she looked at the scar on the back of her right hand and how it rippled as she played.

Jodie abruptly dropped her hands to her lap, one covering the other, the music generating an ache for the losses in her life. Of her mother, when she was only nine. The loss of her plans and dreams in high school. The death of her grandmother a few years ago, and now her father.

She was here for two months. But once those months were done, she was gone. And after that?

She closed the lid on the piano with a *thunk* and got up from the bench. She had learned it never helped to plan too far ahead. That way lay only disappointment and pain.

Finn rode his horse through the corral gate, closed it and then rode up beside Jodie standing by the corral fence. He and Vic had spent a good part of the day gathering Keith's horses from the far pastures of the Rocking M.

Jodie had her arms hooked over the top rail, looking the herd over. Yesterday, at the funeral and later, at the café, she'd seemed shut off. Distant. He put it down to the funeral.

But today she looked more relaxed.

When they'd had arrived at the ranch, Vic had gone up to the house to let her know they were there. To Finn's surprise, Jodie had been waiting at the corrals when they returned with the horses. It had taken some time to get them in the old corrals, and Jodie had helped, opening the gates and closing them behind them.

Now Finn found himself unable to tear his gaze away from her and her thick dark hair shining in the afternoon sun. It flowed over the shoulders of the pink tunic she wore, a flash of bright color against her turquoise-and-purple-patterned skirt. It was the kind of outfit Jodie always favored—different and unusual and just a little out there.

"So how many of these horses belong to my father and how many to Vic?" Jodie asked.

"I think about half of the bunch are Vic's," Finn said, forcing himself to focus on the job at hand, as he dismounted from his horse and tied it up to the fence with a neat bowline knot. It was early afternoon, but the sun was gathering strength.

He and Vic had spent the morning riding the backcountry of the ranch, rounding up Keith's and Vic's horses and herding them into the sketchy corrals. Vic's horses were well behaved enough, but Finn was disappointed to see how wild Keith's had gotten.

Once again he fought down his own regret. He had been too busy with his job as a sheriff's deputy, and working on the side, trying to establish his farrier business, to come regularly. In the past year and a half, the only times he had seen Keith was at the Grill and Chill, where his friend sat at his usual table, drinking coffee and scribbling furiously on pads of paper. Every time

Finn joined him, he would shove the pads in an envelope, as if ashamed.

Now Keith's horses milled in the corral, the close quarters making them reestablish their pecking order. Teeth were bared, heads tossed, ears pinned back, and one or two of the smaller geldings had already been kicked.

"Some of them act pretty wild," Jodie said, dismay in her voice and expression.

"They'll all need some work," Finn stated, pushing his cowboy hat back on his head.

"Work?" Jodie asked.

"Hooves trimmed, for one thing. Could use some grooming. General care. Some round-pen work to settle them down. Some groundwork to retrain them."

Jodie climbed up on the fence, still watching the horses. She seemed more relaxed today than at the funeral. "I recognize a few of them," she said, her smile lighting up her previously somber face. "We used to ride that one. Mickey." She pointed to a bay gelding that was shaking his head and baring his teeth at an appaloosa.

"You might want to be careful on the fence," Finn warned. "The horses are goofy, penned up like this. They've not been worked with for a while."

The words were barely spoken when one of the animals screeched, followed by a resounding thump as hooves connected with hide. Another bared its teeth, kicking at the rails. Then, close to Jodie, a roan mare and a pinto started fighting.

Finn was about to call out to her to get down when both horses reared, hooves flying. The pinto lost its balance and started falling.

Right toward Jodie.

Finn moved fast, hooking his arm around her waist and pulling her back just as the horses fell against the fence. The posts and rails shuddered and Finn prayed they would hold as he spun Jodie around, out of harm's way.

Horses squealed as they struggled to regain their footing. The boards creaked and groaned. Finn looked over his shoulder. Thankfully, the roan scrambled free and galloped away, a couple others in pursuit.

Too close, he thought, relief making his knees tremble.

Then he glanced down at Jodie, realizing that he still had one arm wrapped around her midsection, the other bent over her head. Her hands were clutching his shirt.

"You okay?" he asked, still holding her.

She sucked in a shaky breath, her hair falling into her face as she nodded.

"Thanks. That was kind of scary," she said, her voice wavering.

Finn was lost once again in eyes as blue as the Montana sky above them. As their gazes held, his heart beat faster and his breath became ragged.

Then she blinked and released her grip on him.

As he took a step away from her, he had to force his emotions back to equilibrium, frustrated with his reaction to her. It was as if he had never held a woman in his arms.

He lowered his hands as she pushed her hair away from her face, looking everywhere but at him.

"So, Jodie, you figured out what you want done with your horses?" Vic asked, slapping his dusty hat against his equally dusty blue jeans as he joined them.

Jodie shrugged, looking past Finn to the corrals,

where the horses were slowly settling down. "I'm not sure. I was hoping I could ride one or two of them."

"Today?" Surprise tinged Finn's voice.

"No. Oh, no. I'm not that optimistic," she said with a nervous laugh, obviously still shaken up by her close encounter.

With him or the horses?

Don't flatter yourself, Hicks.

"You did say they were wild," Jodie said.

"So when were you hoping to ride them?" Finn asked.

"I thought in a week or so?" She gave him a tight smile.

"You're here that long?" Her sister was gone, and he'd assumed Jodie would be leaving soon, as well.

"Unfortunately, I'm here for a couple of months."

"If you spend some time with them, you might be able to catch one or two eventually," Vic jumped in before Finn could quiz her. "Your dad let them run wild."

"Even if you catch a few, I wouldn't recommend riding them until you've done some groundwork and round-pen work with them," Finn added. "Settle them down."

"I thought they were trained?"

"So did Finn when we tried to round them up," Vic said with a laugh. "Guess it didn't take."

"It's been a few years since I worked with them," he retorted.

"You trained some of my dad's horses?" Jodie's eyes went wide and her eyebrows hit her hairline. "But you're a deputy."

"He multitasks," Vic said, slapping his hat again, grinning. "Catching crooks by day, horses by night."

"I didn't know you were a trainer," Jodie said to Finn.

"It's something I do on the side."

She nodded, as if storing that information away.

"Tell me what you want done with these cayuses, Jodie," Vic stated, plopping his battered, worn hat on his head. "I'm sorting mine out and loading them up on my trailer. Do you want to move these to the pasture just off the corrals or do you want me to let them go again?"

She caught her lip between her teeth, as if thinking. "I'm not sure what to do. Dad's will said we could offload the moveable assets whenever we wanted. Just not—" She stopped abruptly, waving her hand as if erasing what she'd said.

"Offload as in sell them?" Finn asked in dismay. They were top-notch horses and had some superb bloodlines, though they were a bit wild. It would be a crime to sell them at an auction.

"I can't keep them if I'm not staying, so I guess I'll have to. I should get a decent price. They're good horses. Dad always needed to own the best."

"If you try to sell them right now, you'll only get meat prices for them," Finn said. "The only place you could sell them is at the auction mart."

"So they would get sold for slaughter?" Jodie sounded as concerned as he was. The horses now stood quietly, a sharp contrast to their behavior a few moments ago. The pinto hung her head over the fence, looking almost apologetic.

"Hey, Spotty," she said, walking over, her hand held up. To Finn's surprise, the mare stayed where she was and allowed her to come closer. Jodie rubbed her nose, an expression of such yearning on her face that it caught

Finn off guard. The horse nickered softly, as if respond-
ing to her.

Jodie stroked her neck and then another mare, the
roan, joined them. Spotty stepped to the side, her head
down in submission. Obviously the other mare was
higher up in the pecking order.

"Do you remember me, Roany?" Jodie murmured,
rubbing her nose, as well.

"Some really original names for those horses," Finn
teased. "Roany for a roan, Spotty for a pinto."

"We were city kids. What did we know about proper
horse names?"

"You could have done an internet search," Finn
joked.

Jodie shot him a wry look. "Internet? That complete
waste of time? Besides, back then it would have been
slow dial-up service."

"That's right," Finn mused. "We just got the wire-
less towers in the past few years. Now I can waste time
even faster."

Jodie's light chuckle made him feel better than it
should.

"So when you two are done..." Vic waved as if trying to catch Finn's attention.

"Sorry, Vic," he said, feeling foolish as he turned
away from Jodie. "What do you need?"

"I'll get my horses sorted out and we can load them
up and be out of Jodie's hair," his friend said. "You stay
here with the riding horses. I want to put them on the
trailer last, and these two will get all antsy if I leave
them alone."

Finn wasn't keen on the idea. He knew he should get
going. Jodie had held a dangerous fascination for him

once. But she was too much like his mother, not enough like his beloved Denise.

Before he could object, however, Vic was gone, leaving the two of them alone again.

"So, if you behave, I can take you out in the back pasture," she was saying, still rubbing Roany's nose. "Just like old times."

"You enjoyed riding, didn't you?" Finn asked.

"It was one of the few things I liked about being on the ranch," she countered, stroking Roany. The horse closed her eyes as if reveling in the attention. "Erin and I rode more than Lauren did. I missed it when…" Her voice trailed off again, as if she had other things to say, but either didn't want to or didn't dare.

Which immediately made him curious as to what she'd been planning to say.

"Anyhow, I wouldn't mind going riding again," Jodie was saying. "I'll have nothing but time the next two months."

Finn knew he should let it go, but she'd raised his curiosity. "So why are you staying a couple of months?"

For a few seconds she said nothing, just kept stroking Roany's coat. Then a couple other horses came close, and the mare pinned her ears back and charged at the newcomers.

Jodie stepped away, then wiped her hands on her skirt. "I'm between jobs right now."

"The waitressing one or the playing-piano one?"

"How do you know about that?"

"Your father told me. We did spend a lot of time together at one time." And Keith had always talked of Jodie's occupations with a hint of anger. He was much prouder of Lauren, who had gone on to become a civil engineer, and Erin, who was a graphics designer.

"Both. But I have an opportunity with a band that hopes to start touring soon. They need a pianist and I'm on the short list."

"No plans for settling down?"

Her face grew hard. "No. Not in my destiny."

"And home is Wichita now?"

She frowned in puzzlement. "How did you know?"

"The plates on your car."

"Of course." Jodie sighed, looking back at the house. "For now I'm stuck here, though, thanks to the condition Dad put on the will."

Finn's curiosity won out over his desire to keep her at arm's length. "What condition was that?"

"He wanted each of us girls to stay on the ranch for two months before we could sell it. So I'm doing my duty. Lauren will do hers as soon as possible and we're hoping Erin will come, as well."

Two months? At the ranch?

That the idea created such conflicting emotions both surprised and annoyed him.

Finn couldn't deny that Jodie being around that long held a strong appeal for him. At the same time, she wasn't the type of person he should allow himself to be attracted to, and he knew it deep in his soul.

"So you're positive I'll only get meat prices if I bring these horses to the auction mart in town?" Jodie was asking, turning her attention back to the horses.

Finn nodded, wishing he could detach himself from the thought that these amazing animals would be slaughtered. "I wouldn't make a decision right away, though," he said. "Maybe ask around. See if there's anyone who would be willing to take them."

Jodie nodded again. "For now, it looks as if they need their hooves trimmed. Do you know anyone who could do that for me?"

"I could, if you wanted," he said. He owed that much to Keith.

"That'd be good." Jodie's smile tugged at his resolve to keep his distance from her.

Then Vic was back to grab his riding horses. Time to go.

"I'll see you tomorrow when my shift is over," Finn said to Jodie.

"Stop by the house. I'll give you a hand," she replied.

He nodded, then grabbed his horse's reins and walked over to the horse trailer to load it. But as he did, he couldn't help sneaking a quick glance back to where Jodie still stood.

To his surprise she was watching him, a curious expression on her face.

Chapter Four

She still played piano.

As Finn knocked on the door, familiar music drifted out the open windows of the McCauley house. He remembered his mother playing the piece, but never as frenetically as it was being pounded out now. Yesterday, when he and Vic had come to round up the horses, Jodie had been outside waiting. Did she forget?

But before he knocked again, he listened a moment, feeling sorrowful at the sound. His mother, a pianist herself, had heard Jodie play a few times and praised the young girl's talent. Had talked about mentoring her.

But his mom's reliability was sketchy at best and she'd never followed through on her offer. Just as she'd never followed through on her promises to attend his baseball or basketball games, his school programs or anything requiring her to make a commitment. After his father's death, it was as if she'd lost all her focus on her family. As a result Finn had ended up neglected and alone. It was thanks to Keith McCauley's intervention that he'd had someone who was interested in his well-being. Finn owed Keith more than he could ever repay. The man had been a steadying force in his life.

And it was that history that brought him, reluctantly, here today. Keith's animals needed some basic farrier work. It was the least Finn could do for the man who had been such a huge influence in his life.

He knocked again, more loudly this time.

There was still no answer, so he opened the door and called out, "Anybody home?"

The music stopped abruptly. He heard the screech of a bench being pushed back, then footsteps, and a few seconds later Jodie appeared in the doorway. Today she wore an oversize plaid shirt, a tank top and blue jeans cuffed above bare feet. She had her glossy hair pulled back in a loose braid hanging over one shoulder. She looked more like the country girl he remembered than the retro hippie who'd come to her father's funeral.

"Hey there," she said, folding her arms around her waist. "Glad you could come."

"You got the horses in the corral?" he asked, wanting to get down to business. He had just come off his shift at work and was hungry.

"Sort of," she said, biting her lip. "I couldn't round them all up. Mickey and Roany are still out in the pasture."

"Just as well. I can't trim all their hooves today, anyhow," he said.

"Of course." She slipped on her boots and grabbed a worn straw cowboy hat from a shelf above the empty coatracks.

"I couldn't help hearing the piano," he said, still surprised at the beauty of the music. "You ever play anywhere besides bars?"

"Not much opportunity," she said, dropping the hat on her head and buttoning up her shirt. "And it works for me. Concert pianist was clearly not in the cards."

He felt a nudge of disappointment at how casually she brushed off something she had talked about with such enthusiasm that one summer.

"How did that happen?" When they were dating, the music scholarship was all she'd talked about. When she'd ditched him for a wild party that night and missed her audition the next day, he had been so utterly disappointed both in her and for her. The rest of the summer she'd avoided him and hung out with a bad group. The next summer she hadn't shown up at all, and the only time Keith had mentioned her was to tell Finn about the irresponsible life his youngest daughter was leading.

"Life happens," she said wryly.

Guess that was all he was going to get.

He opened the door for her, but before she walked through, she gave him an enigmatic look. "Still a gentleman, I see."

"One of the few things my mother taught me," he said, following her across the porch.

"Where is she now?" Jodie continued.

"Hopefully on her way to Saddlebank." Finn pushed down the flicker of concern that his mother would flake out on him again. She'd sounded so sincere when she had called him a couple months ago. Maybe things had changed in her life. "She's accompanying Mandie Parker for our church music festival."

"Mandie Parker. I've heard of her."

"Really? She sings Christian contemporary music," Finn said.

Jodie tossed him a wry look. "I'll have you know I have a variety of musical tastes," she stated.

"Sorry, I didn't mean—"

"That I only listen to blues in smoky bars or hip-hop in clubs. I get it."

A smile teased his mouth at her quip. "I stand corrected."

"As for Mandie, it's amazing that you managed to get her. She's very talented."

"The festival's in a couple of weeks. If you're staying here, you could come, if you're interested."

"I just might." Jodie shoved her hands into the back pockets of her blue jeans as she walked alongside him, past the dented and dusty car she had driven here. Clearly waitressing and playing in bars didn't pay enough to buy decent transportation.

"And how is your mother these days?"

"She's doing okay."

"I remember hearing her play at church sometimes when Aunt Laura couldn't. She was so talented. I sometimes wished she could have given me lessons."

"Your grandmother in Knoxville taught you to play, didn't she?"

"She taught all three of us. There wasn't much money for anything else, so she spent her days trying her best to keep us well-rounded and on the straight and narrow."

Finn was sure he didn't imagine Jodie's sardonic tone of voice. "How successful was she?" he couldn't help but ask.

"Well, you did catch me speeding," Jodie replied with a saucy smirk.

"It sounds as though you play as fast as you drive."

"Gramma never let us play outside until we finished

the pieces of music she set out for us. I learned that the sooner I was done with what *she* wanted me to play, the sooner I could play the ones I wanted."

Finn laughed at the mental image of a young girl furiously pounding out the notes to sonatas. "I thought you enjoyed playing the piano? That it was a dream of yours."

Jodie simply shrugged. "I didn't like what Gramma and my mother made me play. Those endless scales and all those boring pieces. Once I mastered them, I enjoyed it more." Her melancholy tone made him wonder again what had happened that she had discarded that dream so callously. "Did your mother teach you, too?" she asked.

"Off and on. I never got the benefit of regular lessons like you did." Or parenting, for that matter.

"Did your mother ever move back here?"

Though she knew what had happened after his father died, Jodie's current interest in his life surprised him. He didn't think she had spared him more than a passing thought after that summer. But it had been another hard day at work, and the conversation was a pleasant antidote.

As was Jodie's company.

"No. She's all over the place right now." And a constant reminder to him of the perils of an undisciplined life.

"And you're not."

"I like Saddlebank. Always have. My dad's family has been here for generations. I want to settle down here."

"You always did like it more than I did."

"It's a good place. And much of the reason I decided to stay had to do with your father. He was a mentor to me. He helped me find my place in the chaos that was my life."

Finn added a smile, hoping his words would give her some comfort. But she looked straight ahead, her hands shoved into the pockets of her jeans as they neared the corrals, the horses whinnying a greeting.

"So what can I do to help you?" Jodie asked, clearly not ready to talk about her father yet.

"Why don't you catch the first horse and bring it out here, and I'll get my trimming equipment," he said.

She nodded and strode over to the hip-roof barn beside the corrals where Keith kept his tack, disappearing inside. A few moments later she stepped into the corral, carrying a halter behind her back. Finn smiled at the old trick, curious to see if it would work.

"Hey, Roany," she said, her voice pitched low and quiet as she approached the large mare, who watched her with curiosity. "Come to Jodie. It's time for your long-overdue pedicure, and if you behave, you might get a carrot when it's over. I know it's supposed to go the other way, first the carrot then the stick, but it's how we like to roll at the Rocking M."

Finn chuckled at her chatter. Jodie could always make people laugh.

He set the large wooden carrier holding his tools by the fence where it couldn't get kicked, and buckled on his heavy leather chaps.

To his surprise, Jodie convinced Roany to come and was already tying up the rope halter, her movements quick and sure.

She petted the horse, mumbled a few more nonsense words to her, then led her out of the corral, quickly moving through the gate and closing it behind her.

"Your first customer," she announced, leading Roany toward him. She leaned her head against the mare's neck, rubbing it on the other side. "And you don't need to tip him," she said to the animal.

As he took the halter, their hands brushed. She jerked back, startling the horse.

"Sorry, Roany. Just a bit jumpy around you yet," she muttered.

But from the way she avoided his gaze, he suspected it wasn't Roany that made her jumpy.

Finn pushed the thought aside, focusing on the hard work that lay ahead. He tied the mare to the hitching post, then ran his hands over her as he walked around her, getting her used to his presence.

Finally he slid his palm up and down her front leg, catching hold of the hock. To his surprise, Roany lifted her hoof.

"Looks as if she still knows her manners," Jodie said.

"Here's hoping she's like that for all her feet," Finn grunted. He bent over, pulled Roany's hoof between his legs and went to work with a pick.

"So you manage to catch up with some old friends the past few days?" he asked, trying to sound casual.

"I didn't have that many close friends when I visited here. Most have left Saddlebank, though I hear Keira, Heather and Lee are all back at Refuge Ranch."

"Yeah. Most of them are married now. Lee and his fiancée, Abby, are tying the knot this summer."

"Good for him. He had a rough go of it, I heard. Went to jail for something he didn't do."

"He's managed to put it behind him, though I can't imagine how." Finn had a hard enough time forgiving his mother for her constant absences in his life. Especially after his father died and Finn had needed her the most.

He returned his attention to Roany.

"You're well behaved," he said to the horse.

"She always was," Jodie agreed. "I loved riding her."

"She was your horse?"

"We spent many hours in the hills together, didn't we, Roany?"

The wistfulness in her voice surprised him. Keith had always given him the impression that Jodie resented coming back here.

"Well, hopefully you can get her settled down enough that you can go riding again."

"I hope so, but I'm not optimistic about her life after this." Jodie's deep sigh made him glance up at her.

"Why do you say that?"

"You may as well know, I asked around and heard that you have a good reputation as a horse trainer and that you seem to have no problem selling the horses you've worked with."

"Thanks for that." He glanced up at her as he lowered Roany's other hoof, wondering where this was going, though he had a fair idea.

"I can't bear the thought of these horses going to the auction market for slaughter. Would you be willing to buy them from me?"

"Sorry, but I don't have room at my place for more horses," he said giving her a look of regret. "And I can't afford to pay what they're worth."

At any other time he would have loved to pick up these animals. They had great bloodlines and would give him a solid foundation for the herd he hoped to build up himself.

"Well, would you have time to train them? Get them into shape so I could sell them? You said it shouldn't take more than a month or two to recondition them."

"No more than that," Finn said, not answering her question, unsure he wanted to think about spending any more time with her.

He recalled that moment yesterday when, for a moment, he'd held her in his arms. He knew the loneliness dogging him since Denise's death was part of the reason he was drawn to Jodie.

But he also knew she held an old attraction he had to avoid.

"I don't think I have time," he said. Between his job, his own horse training and the music festival coming up, he was swamped.

"No time at all?"

He heard the plaintiveness in her voice, but steeled himself against it as he lifted Roany's other front hoof. "Sorry, no. I can give you the name of a few other trainers. But if you and your sisters are selling the ranch, the new owner might want the herd." He couldn't help but think of Vic and his verbal agreement with Keith to eventually buy the ranch. Finn knew his friend had been counting on it, but how would that play out with the terms of Keith's will?

"Maybe, but I don't want to run the risk of them selling the horses for meat. I'd like to know they're going to a good home before I leave."

"I'm sorry, but I can't help you," Finn stated as he set Roany's foot on the stand. He began filing the hoof down, the noise of his hasp the only sound in the peaceful quiet. Jodie climbed onto the fence, watching him.

As Finn worked, he found himself overly aware of

her scrutiny. Of her presence. When he was done, she jumped off the fence.

"You can lead her back now," he said, taking Roany's foot off the stand, then arching his back to get the kink out.

He straightened as Jodie came near and untied the mare from the hitching rail, ducking under her to get to the proper side. As she did, her arm brushed against Finn's, and once again he felt a foolish uptick in his heartbeat as attraction sparked between them.

And he knew she felt it, too, when she glanced away, a flush creeping up her cheeks.

Warning bells sounded in his brain. This girl was a mistake. She would be gone in a couple months.

And he had no desire to be the one left behind again.

Jodie pressed a button to end her most recent call, sighing as she got out of her car, now parked on Main Street.

She had spent most of the day phoning horse trainers and buyers. But it had all been for nothing. She had just finished talking to a horse buyer in Cody passed on to her by another trainer in Billings, whose number Finn Hicks had given her. The buyer in Cody wasn't available to help, nor was she optimistic that Jodie would find someone to purchase the horses if they weren't properly trained.

When her aunt Laura called and asked to meet her at the Grill and Chill for supper, Jodie readily accepted. She felt antsy. Needed to be off the ranch for a while.

The restaurant buzzed with conversations of the late-afternoon crowd as she stepped inside.

"Your aunt is by the windows," Allison Bamford, the

café's waitress, called out as she set an empty pot on the coffee machine, then grabbed an order from the kitchen and bustled away with it. Jodie shouldn't be surprised that Allison knew who she was looking for. This was Saddlebank, the place with no secrets.

She made her way to the table, smiling at the few people who greeted her. She got a few frowns, though, from parents of kids she used to be friends with.

My reputation precedes me, she thought with a pang.

It shouldn't matter to her what the people of Saddlebank thought of her. But the unspoken censure still galled.

"Hello, my dear," Aunt Laura said, getting up from the table. Laura wore her usual sedate shirt, tucked into blue jeans and sensible shoes. "I'm so glad you came to town," she added, hugging her. "I've been so wanting to sit and chat with you."

Jodie returned her hug, holding on a moment longer than necessary, overcome by a peculiar sense of homesickness. After her mother died, living with Gramma had been an exercise in tolerance on both their parts, and staying at the ranch with her father was difficult.

But the occasional stays at Aunt Laura's home in Saddlebank were like an oasis of homemade cookies and hot chocolate and unconditional love. Though she had no children of her own, the woman embraced her nieces and lavished on them the love they'd lost when their mother died.

Aunt Laura pulled away, puzzlement etched on her features. "Is everything okay, sweetie?"

"It is now," Jodie said, waiting for her aunt to sit down before she did.

Allison came by with coffee and menus, but Jodie

knew what she wanted. "I'll have Gord's loaded burger with a side of onion rings," she said.

"You still eating that unhealthy food?" Aunt Laura said with a grimace.

"Only when I'm in Saddlebank," she replied. "It's the mountain air that gives me the appetite for trans fats."

Laura ordered fish and vegetables, slanting Jodie a questioning look as if giving her an opportunity to change her mind.

"I'll stick with the fried stuff," she said to Allison.

"So how does it feel to be back here?" her aunt asked, leaning forward on the table when the waitress left. "Not too many bad memories?"

"Some." She didn't say more than that. "But it's over now."

"Now that your father is dead." Laura sighed, then took Jodie's hands in hers. "I know he wasn't the best man in the world, but he was still your father."

"I know that," Jodie said, interrupting her. "And that's the thing I struggle with. How I feel about a man who was my father. I should feel sadder that he's gone, but the truth is, I didn't see him much after I left."

"I wish you could have talked to him before he died. Might have given you some closure. He spent a lot of time here toward the end, sitting at his usual table by the door, scribbling on pieces of paper." Laura smiled at her. "Not sure what he was working on, but it kept him busy."

Probably various versions of the addendum to the will, Jodie thought. "It might have helped. Dad and I had a complicated relationship."

"I know. And I know he struggled with it."

Jodie bit back a response to that. "Anyhow, thanks to

Dad's will, each of us girls has to stay at the ranch two months before we can sell it," she explained.

"Sell?" The horrified look on her aunt's face made her realize how blunt her words sounded. "You want to sell the ranch? It's been in McCauley hands for two generations, and Bannisters before that. You can't sell…" Her aunt's voice faded away and regret lanced Jodie.

"I'm sorry, Aunt Laura," she said, still clinging to her hands. "But I can't stay here forever. There's nothing here for me. Except you, but I can still come and visit. Besides, the decision isn't only mine. Erin and Lauren both agree."

"How is Erin? She didn't come to the funeral."

"I'm worried about her, but she told Lauren that she'll come when it works for her."

"She's always been such a sweet, tenderhearted girl. I sure hope she's okay."

So do I, thought Jodie.

"So what has been keeping you busy at the ranch the past few days?" her aunt asked.

Jodie quickly latched on to the change in topic. "I've been trying to find someone to train the animals so I can sell them as riding horses instead of them going for slaughter. I asked Finn if he could, but he said he's busy."

"Really?" Her aunt tilted her head to one side. "That's too bad. I heard he's a good horse trainer, as well as being a good deputy. A multitalented man. Your father liked him. Didn't you two date at one time?"

Jodie ignored the question, choosing to concentrate on getting the perfect amount of sugar into her coffee. Finn had been the one bright spot in that horrible summer. Now they were so far apart in their individual journeys there was no way they'd have anything in common anymore.

"Well, well, speaking of…" Aunt Laura said, looking past Jodie, her smile widening.

"Good afternoon, Miss McCauley. Jodie." The deep voice beside their table made Jodie jump. Her gaze tangled with a pair of hazel eyes. Finn Hicks stood by their table, still in uniform, one hand resting on a belt weighed down by hardware, the other holding his hat. The hint of a smile on his face created a silly flutter in her heart.

Plus it didn't hurt that the stubble shadowing his cheeks emphasized his cheekbones and the dent in his strong chin.

"Sorry to bother you," he said. "But I'd like to talk to you, Miss McCauley. Laura McCauley, that is," he corrected.

Jodie's aunt seemed taken aback, looking from Finn to Jodie as if wondering why he wanted to talk to her instead of her niece. "Well, pull up a chair. Did you want anything to eat? I'm buying," she said.

"No. Thanks. Sorry again to interrupt. I won't be but a minute," he said, shooting an apologetic look at Jodie as he pulled a chair from a table beside them. But as he sat down, their knees brushed and Jodie jumped back at the contact.

"So what can I do for you?" Aunt Laura asked, her smile widening as she looked from one to the other. Jodie wasn't sure she liked her aunt's eager expression.

Finn scratched his chin with his forefinger, glancing again at Jodie, then to her aunt. "You know we've got that church music festival coming up. I'm on the committee."

"It's the talk of the town. I'm excited about hearing your mother play, but more than that, to hear Mandie sing," Laura said.

"That's why I need to talk to you. My mom called today and said she has some other commitment and won't be able to come." Finn blew out a sigh, his features grim. "I need a new accompanist. I had hoped you could help me."

Aunt Laura shook her head. "There's no way I'm nearly accomplished enough to play for Mandie." She flicked a glance at Jodie, her smile growing. "But my niece is."

Jodie stared at her. What was she up to? And then she caught the gleam in her aunt's eye and everything clicked.

She turned to Finn and dashed the hope she saw on his face. "Sorry. The only place I've played the past few years is in bars, and I doubt you'd want to bring me before the church board."

Finn's expression hardened just a bit, which convinced her even more that she wasn't doing this.

"But, honey, it's a wonderful opportunity," Aunt Laura was saying. "Mandie is internationally known. She might be able to help you with your own musical career."

Jodie entertained the thought for a moment, her old dreams rising up from the ashes. Then she shook it off. She didn't have the best résumé to accompany a Christian contemporary singer. "That ship has sailed, Aunt Laura. I've got other plans."

"Like what?"

Jodie let her question sit, unanswered. She wasn't

sure what her other plans were. Up until now her goals were work, travel, work, travel.

She knew that she wasn't keen on spending more time with Finn than was necessary. Though it had been years, he resurrected feelings she hadn't experienced in a while. Feelings of hope for a life she had always yearned for.

Plus, Finn had been Keith's friend, and she still couldn't reconcile their connection with her own tumultuous relationship with her father.

Finn dragged his hand over his face. "Do you know anyone else who could help me?" he asked, turning back to Aunt Laura, clearly as unwilling to press Jodie as she was to help him out.

Laura sat back in her chair, arms folded. "No. There isn't anyone around here capable enough of playing for someone of Mandie's caliber. Your mother would have been ideal, but seeing as she can't make it, you don't have much choice left." Then her eyes took on a speculative gleam that made Jodie's neck prickle. "So here's what I think would work. Finn, you need someone to play for you, and Jodie is perfect for the job. Jodie, you need someone to train your horses, and Finn is perfect for that job. Why don't you two come to an amicable trade?"

The prickle on Jodie's neck grew as she glanced over at Finn in time to catch him looking at her. He seemed as wary as she felt, but she also saw a tiny spark of hope.

"You could help each other out. It's a win-win," Aunt Laura said.

Jodie tried to imagine herself playing in church in front of the members, but the picture wouldn't gel. She didn't belong there.

But weighted against that was the thought that her beloved horses would not be headed for slaughter if she agreed.

Still, she hesitated, glancing again at Finn. Their eyes met and once more she felt that unwelcome spark.

"I guess this could work." But even as she spoke the words, a dissenting voice deep in her soul told her she was making a mistake.

"Then, that's settled. I'll leave it up to you two to hash out the arrangements," Aunt Laura said with a satisfied tone.

Then, thankfully, Allison was there with their food.

"And I'll leave you two to your supper." Finn got up and set his chair at the table beside them. "Guess we'll be in touch," he said to Jodie.

Was it her imagination or did he sound as enthusiastic about the trade as she did?

She gave him a weak smile, then looked down at her hamburger.

It would be okay, she told herself as she squirted ketchup on her plate. She knew who she was and who Finn was. She wasn't about to open herself up to heartbreak again.

Chapter Five

"I hope Jodie comes soon," Amy Bernstein sighed, tapping the envelope holding the sheet music against her thigh in time with her toe tapping on the stage floor. Amy was a member of the committee putting on the church music festival and had insisted on being present when Jodie played. Finn understood her concerns. No one had ever heard Jodie perform and Mandie Parker was too big a name to leave things to chance. She glanced at her phone, which she then slipped into a large leather bag. "I need to leave by five thirty. I've had a long day at work."

"She said she would be here and I believe her," Finn said, shooting an exasperated glance at the clock on the back wall of the church sanctuary, wondering if he had made a mistake.

Now each tick of the clock increased the pressure he felt. Finn had specifically told Jodie that they had to meet at the church at four thirty to run through the music Mandie had sent them. It was getting closer and closer to five.

"If she can't be punctual for something like this, I

have grave concerns about the actual concert," Amy said as she sat down on the piano bench, crossing one slender leg over the other and clasping her hands around her knees. Her tailored suit was barely wrinkled even after a day of work at the bank. "Jodie has had, how shall I say, an unstable lifestyle after she left here."

"What do you mean?"

The woman waved a manicured hand. "I'm sorry. I shouldn't have said anything. I'm sure you know the whole sad story of her life. You and Keith were quite close."

"Keith was good to me," Finn admitted.

Amy sighed, shaking her head at the tragedy of it all. "That poor man lost out on so much when his wife left him. And those girls. Such a messed-up childhood. I'm sure that's why Jodie became the wild girl she did."

Finn easily remembered the "wild girl" Amy referred to. Jodie's descent into partying that summer had bothered him on so many levels, but she wouldn't talk to him about it and had avoided him at all costs the last few weeks she was here.

He'd gotten over it, of course, and thanks to Keith, found the perfect girl in Denise. Uncomplicated and a strong Christian.

But more and more Finn realized he'd never quite gotten over their high school romance.

The sound of the outside door shutting echoed through the building. He heard hurried footsteps down the hallway, then Jodie appeared at the entrance of the sanctuary. She paused there, looking around as if getting her bearings.

Finn caught a fleeting expression of sorrow on her

features, but it was chased away by a strained smile as her eyes fell on the two of them.

"I'm so glad you could finally make it, Jodie," Amy said, her tone coolly polite. "We need to get started right away. I have to be home soon."

"Sorry," Jodie replied, breathless as she hurried down the aisle, pulling down the sleeves of her thin sweater. It floated around her like the wings of a butterfly. He caught glimpses of little ribbon roses embroidered on it matching the bright red of her capri pants. Fun and funky. Only Jodie could pull off an outfit like that.

"I was out riding Roany and I forgot to take my watch or my phone," she continued.

"What happened to you?" He frowned, seeing the small cut on her temple.

Jodie's hand flew to her head. "Oh. Nothing. I just… Clumsy, you know."

As she raised her arm, he noticed a large purple bruise on her forearm through the fine fabric of her sweater. "So what actually happened?"

"It's nothing. I told you." She hurriedly lowered her arm, her cheeks flushing. Her anger puzzled him, but finally he put everything together.

"Did Roany throw you?"

She lifted her chin, her eyes flashing. "I thought she would be okay. After how good she was when you were trimming her hooves. Thought I could do some training myself."

Finn was about to make another comment when Amy noisily cleared her throat, a not-so-subtle hint that time was ticking away.

"I have the music here," the woman said, picking

up the envelope she had laid on the piano bench. She gave Jodie a warm smile. "It's good to see you again, sweetie."

"Good to see you, too." But Jodie didn't meet her eyes as she pulled the sheet music from the envelope.

Finn was surprised at Jodie's reserved response to the friendly overture. Amy seemed to be as well, her brows meeting in a brief frown quickly replaced by a gentle smile.

"I hope this isn't too much for you," she said, touching Jodie lightly, as if trying to make a connection.

"I can manage," Jodie stated, looking over the papers, all business now, but still ignoring Amy's overture.

Something was off, Finn thought, trying to figure out why Jodie was so cool to Amy, who seemed willing to help.

He glanced over Jodie's shoulder at the music. "Doesn't look too complicated," he said.

"I don't think so, either. The key on this one seems high, though." She frowned as she flipped through the sheets of music. "What do you think?"

But she addressed her question to Finn, not Amy.

"Why do you say that?" he wondered.

"Mandie has a deeper voice that might be straining on these high notes. I'm surprised she would want to do it in this key."

"You've listened to her sing?" Finn was surprised but yet thankful that Jodie had done some homework.

"I downloaded most of her songs onto my phone to prepare myself," she said. "I'd like to talk to her about this."

"If you have anything to say to Mandie, I prefer

that you go through me," Amy interjected, her tone unyielding.

"If I'm playing for Mandie, wouldn't it be easier if I spoke to her myself?"

"I'm sorry, my dear." Amy gave Jodie a benevolent smile. "I know you mean well, but we prefer to have as few people as possible talking to her. Mandie is a busy woman and we can't have her distracted by pointless questions."

Jodie laughed, but Finn heard an underlying nervousness. Again he was puzzled at the relationship between the two.

"I can't believe talking to the person accompanying her would be distracting," Jodie said.

"We're just trying to be considerate of her time." This was accompanied by an obvious glance at the clock. "Even though you will be playing today, we still haven't made a final decision on who is to accompany Mandie."

Jodie sent Finn a puzzled look. "I thought you needed me?"

"We do. For now. But if Finn's mother shows up, we might not." Amy folded her hands together. "Christie McCauley is a very talented player." This compliment was directed at Finn, who couldn't argue with that, but who wasn't sure Amy's faith in his mother was justified.

"My mom specifically called me to tell me she couldn't come," he said with a note of finality. "I doubt that will change. Jodie, why don't you try the songs out?"

Finn guessed there was more to their conversation than what he was hearing, but he wasn't about to get sidetracked by a history he knew nothing about.

"Play them a couple of times and we can see how comfortable you are with the pieces," Finn said.

Jodie clenched her hand, then sat on the piano bench, wincing as she did so.

Which made Finn wonder how badly she'd been hurt when she was thrown.

But she rested her hands on the keyboard, took a long, slow breath and squared her shoulders.

Then began to play.

The notes pouring from the piano filled the vast emptiness of the sanctuary, echoing with a harmony that made him shiver.

As Jodie played, Finn saw the tension that had been gripping her loosen. A half smile played over her lips and she canted her head to one side, rocking in time to the music. Then she began to improvise, letting the tune rise up, playing with the timing.

Finn watched her, his own smile growing as he saw another side of the Jodie he remembered making an appearance. Sweet, kind and loving, utterly lost in the music she performed.

"Excuse me," Amy said with a nervous laugh, her hands fluttering in protest. "Stop. Please. That's not how the song goes."

Jodie's fingers fell on the keys in a discordant note. "Sorry," she said. "Just got carried away."

"Of course you did," Amy said. "But this isn't the time or place. This is Mandie's music and you should play it the way she has it laid out. This is a church function, my dear. Not a piano bar." The woman's smile seemed to grow more forced with each passing minute.

"I realize that," Jodie said, starting to get up from the

piano, all the previous joy seemingly leeched out of her face. "I'm sorry to have wasted your time."

"Wait a minute," Finn said, putting his hand on her shoulder to stop her, feeling a moment of panic. If she left, he'd have no one to accompany the singer. "I think Jodie was simply playing around with the music," he said. "Just being creative."

"That may be, but the purpose of an accompanist is to accompany. Not lead where she decides to go," Amy said, the voice of reason.

"Naturally." Finn glanced at Jodie, who still sat at the piano. "And you'll play it the way Mandie wants, right?"

She nodded, flipping through the rest of the music.

"So why don't you try one of the other ones?" he suggested, trying to keep the peace.

Jodie sighed and Finn saw she wasn't happy, but she played the next piece, hitting each note with deliberate perfection. At the same time, there was no life or personality to it.

Nor was it as fun to see her playing.

Amy smiled in approval. "That's much better. Can you play the other pieces as well before I leave? I want to be out of here ASAP. My time does have value, you know."

"A TiVo would make things easier for you," Jodie said, her tone casual.

Finn was completely lost. Where did that come from?

Looking from Jodie's challenging expression to Amy's now narrowed eyes, he wasn't sure he wanted to know.

"You haven't changed a bit," the older woman said, her voice holding a harsh edge that seemed out of proportion to the conversation.

She stood aside, arms crossed, fingers tapping as Jodie ran through the rest of the music.

As soon as Jodie was done, Amy swept down the aisle without a backward glance.

The sudden slamming of the outside door echoed like a gunshot in the silence Amy left in her wake. Jodie fought down her frustration. Even after these years, that woman still got her going.

"So what was that all about?" Finn asked, his puzzlement showing on his features.

Jodie looked back at him, feeling again the touch of his hand on her forehead. How it raised unwelcome and yet irresistible feelings of attraction.

"It was a flip comment. I shouldn't have said it."

"But now you have me curious."

She didn't want to say anything, but she could tell he wouldn't leave her alone until he satisfied his curiosity.

"Amy has to be home on time to watch her favorite television show," she said with a shrug, feeling petty. "It comes on at six. She never misses it."

"Hence the TiVo comment."

"I shouldn't have said that," Jodie replied. "It was unkind."

"I'm guessing you know her schedule because you and her daughter used to be friends?"

"Yes. We hung out when we lived here. Like you and I, Clair and I had…we had a falling out."

Which was a kind way to explain their huge blowup that summer.

"About what?"

Jodie flushed a little, remembering the mixture of

guilt and thrill she had felt when Finn had asked her out, knowing that Clair had had a crush on him for years.

"You're blushing. What happened?"

She lifted her hands and let them fall. "You happened. You asked me out and she didn't like it, because she had 'claimed' you as hers. I broke a cardinal girl-friend rule when I went out with you."

"Girlfriend rule?"

"You never accept a date with a guy your friend has a crush on. Except Clair was an odd kind of friend."

"How so?"

"We'd hang out and be really close, and then a week later, I'd be ignored and left out. The usual girl drama. I'd go home to Knoxville, come back for the summer and I'd be the new, fun friend again. When we got older, we used to sneak out and go to parties together." Jodie gave him an apologetic smile. "Not exactly what I'd like you to know about me."

"And Amy blames you for that?"

Jodie turned back to the piano, idly noodling out a tune, trying to find the best way to say what she wanted to. "When Clair found out I was dating you, she was furious. And later that summer, she partied a lot. She never really got out of that lifestyle after she moved away. Amy seems to think that's my fault."

Jodie tried to leave the past where it belonged. Thankfully, Finn didn't ask any more questions, so she turned to him.

"So what did you think? Do we still have a deal? Will I be accompanying Mandie and will you be training my horses?"

"Yes, we have a deal, if you're still willing."

"Yes." In spite of Amy, she knew she didn't have much choice.

"And Amy just wanted to hear you herself. For one reason or another she didn't like the idea of you playing."

"So was she serious?" Jodie asked instead. "About me not being able to talk to Mandie?"

"I can give you Mandie's number if you think anything needs to change," Finn said.

Relief loosened the tension in Jodie's shoulders. For a moment she'd thought he was siding with Amy. But knowing that Finn had her back meant more than she'd realized.

"I don't want to change anything," Jodie said, getting up. "I just want to go over a few things with her. Get a feel of what she wants to do."

Finn nodded as he got up as well, and they stood across from each other, as if unsure what else to say.

"Well, I better—"

"So how was—"

"Sorry."

"Go ahead…"

Jodie chuckled at their truncated conversation. "Please, why don't you go first?"

Finn laughed as well, his eyes crinkling at the corners, teasing lines appearing at the edges of his mouth. "I was just wondering what set Roany off when you went riding. So I know what to work with her on."

"I'm not sure. I was out in the pasture with the other horses, which was a mistake. One of them came toward us and Roany spun and bucked. It was completely out of the blue."

"You didn't get hurt too badly?"

"My pride more than anything," Jodie said with a light laugh, downplaying what had actually happened. "The thought of arriving late bothered me more."

She had an obstinate desire to prove her dependability to him. That had been her biggest inducement to catch an agitated Roany and climb back on. The ride back to the ranch had been a wild and painful one, with Roany bucking a few more times, the other horses converging on them and challenging them. But at least she'd made it.

"I was thinking of coming tomorrow after work to start on the horses," Finn was saying. "If that's okay with you?"

"Sure. What time does your shift end?"

"About five thirty."

"Okay. Sounds good. I'll see you then."

She had to bite back the urge to invite him for supper. Being around Amy was too stark a reminder of the impossibility of that situation.

This was strictly a business proposition. Jodie was helping him with the festival. He was helping her with the horses.

Best not to blur the lines.

Chapter Six

"I know you want to talk, Roany," Finn said, tossing the rope he held toward the horse. "Just focus on me and this will all be over soon."

The only sounds that could be heard in the silence were the steady beat of Roany's hooves in the dirt, the occasional clucking from Finn to encourage her.

Jodie sat perched on the top rail of the fence, her attention split between Roany and the man standing in the middle of the round pen, following the horse's movements as it ran around the perimeter. His cowboy hat shaded his face from the warm afternoon sun and he had rolled up the sleeves of his twill shirt. His faded blue jeans and worn cowboy boots held smudges from the dust of the pen.

Today he looked more approachable. Less like the sheriff's deputy, more like a man she could spend time with.

He was patient, she thought. Her father would have been yelling long ago, but Finn kept his movements slow and deliberate, flicking the rope at the horse, talking to her in a modulated voice.

"When are you going to let her stop?" Jodie asked, resting her hands on the sun-warmed wood beside her, intrigued by Finn's patience.

"When she shows her willingness to talk to me. Until then, she's got to keep going."

He glanced up at her, their eyes meeting for a brief moment, then looked away, his attention back on the horse.

Jodie swallowed down her reaction. She was attracted to him, but always, behind that, was a feeling of vulnerability. Unworthiness. She couldn't put herself in that position again. Given her history with her father and Lane, her walls were up pretty high.

But this is Finn.

When his truck had pulled up into the yard an hour ago, Jodie had struggled between the need to be out here helping him and the desire to stay away. To protect herself from feelings that were taking root. But when she saw him ambling across the pasture toward Roany, hands at his side, dangling the halter rope, easy and calm, she couldn't stop the unwelcome uptick of her heartbeat.

But a deal was a deal, so she had given herself a stern talking-to about how she was here for only a short while. How she had a once-in-a-lifetime opportunity to go touring with a band.

So why did the thought of traveling for six months not give her the pleasure it once had? Why did the ranch, a place she used to hate, seem to be calling her to stay, rest and catch her breath?

"So why do you keep her moving?" she asked, stifling her dangerous thoughts.

You've got to look out for yourself because no one else will.

"I'm simulating what happens in the pasture with the other horses, using their language. They all chase and push each other until one yields. Roany is the top horse and so she'll have a harder time surrendering to me, but you'll see it when she does. I'm letting her realize that I'm the boss. When she finally understands, I'll reward her." He laughed lightly then, firing Jodie an apologetic glance. "Sorry. Talking too much."

"No. This is interesting. My dad's method of training was increasing the decibels."

"I have a hard time seeing that. I learned quite a bit from him."

Finn's comment underlined the disconnect between her father's public persona and his private one. Finn's perception of him versus Jodie's. So, again, she didn't elaborate.

Roany turned her head toward him, then dropped it just enough, her tongue working her lips.

"Good girl," Finn said, lowering the rope and standing perfectly still. Roany came toward him and he rewarded her by petting her. "See what she did with her mouth? That was her way of showing her submission to me. It's how horses out in the pasture or in the wild talk to each other, as well."

"So now what do you do?"

"Now we work the other side. Keep a balance." He turned Roany around and got her moving again, in the other direction. But this time it didn't take as long for her to submit, and soon he was rewarding her. "Horses want to please us. They simply need to know what we want."

"Well, I certainly didn't want to end up on the ground yesterday," Jodie said. Her leg was still sore, the scrape on her forehead still stinging. "I somehow thought that she would remember me and listen better."

"Roany was feeling snorty the other day. Horses need constant work. They're always testing you. I should have warned you. I'm sorry."

"You don't need to apologize for my dumb choices," Jodie said.

"Why don't you come down from that fence? Talk to her yourself?"

"Are you sure? I don't want to interfere."

"If I was starting from scratch, I wouldn't let you in here, but because I'm only reteaching what she knows, it doesn't hurt for you to be involved. Especially if you figure on riding her again. And I think you should."

"By myself?"

"No. But I'd like to take her out and work with her on a trail. We can go tomorrow when I'm done with work. I'd like to ride her myself, make sure she's relearned some of her lessons."

"So which horse would I ride?"

"I'll bring one of mine. Then you can see what a well-trained horse is like to ride, and watch me work with Roany."

The thought of going out into the hills, where she had initially been headed with Roany, tugged at Jodie's emotions. She had missed riding while she'd been away. Missed the freedom she felt in the quiet, open spaces.

And spending some time with Finn?

Had nothing to do with it.

"Okay. That sounds good."

"I'll let you know when I can come." He gestured

to her. "But for now you still need to establish some authority with this horse if you ever want to ride her again."

Still she hesitated, because she didn't want Finn to see how stiff she was from her ride and her fall yesterday, and because she had promised herself that she would keep her distance from him.

"She'll be fine. You don't need to be afraid."

The word *afraid* stung her McCauley pride. And that forced her to jump off the fence, all the while struggling to ignore the pain shooting through her leg.

Finn's scowl told her how unsuccessful she had been.

"You okay?"

"Just out of shape," she said, forcing a smile to cover up the wince.

"Are you sure?" He tipped his head to one side, gently brushing her hair away from her forehead. She knew it was a casual gesture, but it felt too good. It had been a long time since anyone besides her sisters cared how she was doing. She didn't like how it created another tiny connection between them.

"This scrape looks better," he said, the concern in his voice and his touch resurrecting the same emotions they had the other day.

"It's fine. Just have to be extracareful with the hair flatiron," she joked, pulling back, trying to inject a casual note into a conversation veering into dangerous territory. "It'll heal and give me a story to tell my friends when I leave."

"Of course." His tone was abrupt. As if he was disappointed.

You're reading more into this than is safe. You know how life works.

The voice of reality grounded her and made her focus on Roany, who watched her as if waiting for some signal of what she wanted.

"So what do you want me to do?"

"Just talk to her. Then we'll do some pressure and release work."

Jodie took the lead rope and stroked Roany's nose. "Okay, so I'm hoping you won't toss me off again if we spend some time together here," she said to the horse. "You realize that I don't quite trust you. Twice thrown—"

"She threw you twice?"

"Once up in the pasture, and then later on, as we headed home."

"Why didn't you tell me that?"

"Didn't think it was necessary."

"Sounds as though I'll need to refocus on basic discipline and reward."

"That seems harsh," Jodie said, keeping her attention on the mare, trying to stifle her awareness of Finn as he stepped closer, his arm brushing hers as he took Roany's halter from her.

"Mostly it's about guidance. Making it easy for her to do what you want her to, and hard for her to do what she prefers."

"Basically, then, it's about punishment?" Seemed as if Finn was like her father after all. "The law enforcement part of Finn Hicks coming out?"

He slanted her a look of disapproval. "You make it sound as if that's a bad thing."

Jodie wrapped her arms around her midsection, taking a step away from him. "I spent two months of every year living with the long arm of the law."

The day that she'd decided to not come to the ranch was the day she'd promised herself her father would have no more influence over her life. She had made her own choice and she had chosen not to see him.

"Your dad was always quite proud of being a sheriff," Finn said, taking her comment at face value. "I was always surprised he didn't sell the ranch and stick to law."

"He inherited the ranch from his father, who was a cousin to the Bannisters. They are the family who own the ranch that celebrated their one-hundred-and-fifty-year anniversary last year."

"I noticed you didn't come home for that," Finn said.

"I was busy. And I was never as close to my distantly related cousins as Lauren was." Also, she'd been working, saving up for her next trip, and had had no desire to see her father. "But I think my dad always felt that he couldn't sell a place full of family history."

"But you'll sell it?"

"The place holds no amazing memories for me," she admitted.

Finn nodded, walking slowly back and forth as he led Roany through what looked like a pattern. "No good memories at all?"

"I have some that aren't part of the ranch. Why do you ask?"

He shot her a glance, a smile lifting one corner of his mouth. "I guess I'd just like to know what makes you tick."

Why did that matter to him?

She couldn't let herself think too much about that. Instead, she reached out and patted Roany, establishing her own connection with the animal, her resistance to Finn wearing away under his quiet insistence.

Pressure and release.

The thought flitted through her mind and she smiled.

"What's so funny?"

She shook her head, looking over at him. "I feel like you're using your horse-training tactics on me."

"All part of my charm."

Her smile grew as she tucked her hair behind her ear.

"I made some bad mistakes that summer," Jodie said, going back to their original conversation. "I wish…I wish things had turned out differently."

His eyes caught hers and for a moment awareness arced between them.

"I do, too." That was all he said before turning back to the horse.

Finn led Roany around the pen, his heart beating faster at Jodie's last comment.

He felt as if he and she hovered on the edge of some unnamed territory.

Did he dare go there? She was leaving soon. He felt as if he had to remind himself of that.

Finally his curiosity won out. "So what happened back then?" he asked.

"That summer I stood you up?"

He tossed her a look over his shoulder, adding a grin. "The summer you tore my heart into a million little pieces, then tossed them out the window of your life."

She laughed, as if relieved. "You seem to have recovered."

"I'm resilient."

"So I hear. You even got engaged."

He was surprised she knew. But then this was Saddlebank. There were no secrets in this town.

He nodded. "Yes. Denise." Saying her name brought the usual note of grief. However it seemed to be diminishing as time went by.

Especially the past few days.

"Can I ask what happened to her?" Jodie asked.

"She died a couple of months after we got engaged."

"I'm so sorry. I didn't know that."

He gave Jodie a reassuring smile. "It happened four years ago. She was a nurse, a lovely person. Very strong in her faith. Very involved in the church. In fact, it was thanks to your father that we got together. He met her at the hospital in Bozeman when he escorted a prisoner there. She was so compassionate, he said. He encouraged me to date her and I was glad I did."

"She sounds like the perfect match for you."

"She was. I loved her a lot." He glanced Jodie's way, wanting to bridge the gap stretching between them since she'd left. "How about you? You meet anyone?"

She fiddled with the hem of her sweater. "I did. He wasn't involved in church, though he was a good person."

"What happened?"

"We had a falling out."

Her words were sparse, as if they still caused her pain.

"Now *I'm* sorry."

She shrugged. "He wasn't the right person for me. And I made some mistakes, as usual. Some of the decisions I'd made I should have thought through better."

"Like your decision not to go for your audition?" he asked.

"That decision was taken out of my hands," she said. "Literally."

"What do you mean?" Finn made another round with Roany, then led her to the gate leading to the pasture. He had done enough work with her for now. Time for a break.

"I don't want to talk about it," Jodie said, her voice quiet but determined.

"You're leaving soon," he replied, fighting down his frustration. "Why don't you tell me? I'd really like to know what happened."

Jodie sighed, her eyes flicking from him to Roany. "What does it matter? That was a long time ago."

"Call it male pride," he said with a light laugh, determined to show her that he was simply interested. Nothing more. "I guess I'd like to know why you didn't want to go on that date with me." And why, instead of going out with him, she'd been hanging around the next day with Jaden, of all people.

"If you really want to know, I was pretty happy when you asked me out. You were a good guy." She busied herself unlatching the gate, her hair falling over her face, hiding her expression. "I really enjoyed our dates together. And later that summer when I got the call for the audition, it seemed too good to be true. I guess I hardly dared believe something good could happen to me. I was kind of mixed up about what I wanted to do. Going for the audition made me nervous. Thinking about getting serious with you even more."

"I can't imagine you nervous about anything."

"Well, I was, after we had gone out a couple of times. I knew things were getting, well, more serious. And then, because I was nervous, I made another dumb decision when I want to the party at Jaden's. I remember sitting there, thinking about you and about the audition, and realized what I was doing was crazy. I didn't need to live like this. I had good things to look forward to…"

She let the sentence trail off, and Finn wondered if she included him as part of the positive things. But he said nothing, leading Roany through the gate, waiting while Jodie came through herself and latched the gate behind them. She leaned against the fence while he unbuckled the halter.

"Good job, girl," he murmured to Roany, then patted her on the shoulder.

The mare tossed her head once, as if letting him know he may have gotten the best of her this time, but they would meet again. Then she ran off.

Finn coiled up the rope, walking back to Jodie, sensing she had more to say.

"So what happened when you came to that realization?"

"My dad arrived to bust up the party. I was the first person he saw when he stepped inside. He didn't give me a chance to explain that I was leaving, that I hadn't been drinking. He got angry, told me I didn't deserve to even think about you." She looked down at her hands, weaving her fingers together. Finn saw the scar on the back of her right hand and remembered her walking around town the next day with a bandage on it.

"As usual, I had a fight with my dad. He was furious, grounded me, and I missed my date with you," she said, her voice subdued. "I skipped out on my audition and went to another party in the middle of the day. I do believe I saw you that day."

"Yeah, you were with Jaden."

"We weren't dating, in case you were wondering. Just hanging out. Being stupid."

Truth be told, Finn was surprised at how relieved that confession made him feel.

"I spent that whole summer in a haze of stupidity and bad decisions," she said. "I knew you were disappointed with me, but I figured I had blown my chance with you already, so what did it matter? The summer after that, when I was supposed to come here, I got off the bus early. Never made it to Montana and never went back to Knoxville."

As she related the events of that time, he heard the sorrow for the loss of her dreams. He still sensed she'd left something out, but hearing her version of what had happened made a big difference for him. She hadn't ditched him after all. She'd been grounded.

Finn couldn't help himself; he touched her shoulder. Then she covered his hand with hers. It was cold, and he wrapped his fingers around it.

"So what did you do after that? You didn't graduate high school, did you?"

She shook her head, tugging on her hand. But he didn't let it go, gently stroking his thumb over her fingers, maintaining the connection between them.

Something told him he was making a mistake. She wasn't the kind of girl he was looking for. Yet in her haunted expression he saw the girl he had once cared for.

"I managed. I supported myself. I never had to ask anyone for help. Least of all my father," she said in a defiant tone. Finn saw the anger in her eyes. "And now, thanks to Keith willing me a third of this place, I have a chance to do something with my life."

"You mean something *else*," Finn said carefully.

"Knowing you, you've already done something worthwhile."

She held his gaze a moment, then pulled her hand free. "Thanks for the vote of confidence, but it's misplaced." Then she gave him a tight smile. "So will I see you tomorrow?"

"Of course. Like I said, I'll bring one of my horses for you to ride."

"I'm looking forward to it."

Finn met her eyes, and to his surprise, she didn't look away.

He felt his breath quicken and his pulse follow suit.

She looked so lost.

She gave him a half smile and he caught a hint of sorrow in her eyes. A touch of pain.

Over what had happened between them all those years ago?

He reached out and brushed a strand of hair away from her face, then cupped her chin in his palm.

Her eyes widened as she covered his hand with hers, then she swallowed hard and pulled away.

"I should go," she whispered as she turned.

Finn watched her leave, his own emotions in flux.

That was a mistake.

And yet he wondered if it truly was.

Chapter Seven

"You sure I'll be okay on that beast?" Jodie eyed with distrust the large brown quarter horse that Finn had finished saddling by the corrals. As promised, he had shown up with his horse this morning. Before he came, Jodie had picked up the phone any number of times to call off their ride.

After their moment yesterday in the corral, she'd found herself touching her cheek where Finn's rough hand had held it.

It isn't a good idea. Going riding wasn't part of the deal. You could call it off.

But she didn't. Instead, she went into her father's office and spent the rest of the afternoon and evening cleaning up. She felt like an intruder and had to work up her courage to step inside, but the job needed to be done and she needed to keep busy.

But spending time in the office didn't help her fluctuating emotions, either.

Finn had been a good friend of her dad's. He admired him.

She should stay away.

But she had her own memories of Finn, and it was those memories that had kept her from canceling, creating a flutter of anticipation at the thought of going riding with him.

"His name is Henry, and yes, you'll be fine," Finn grunted as he pulled the cinch tight. With a few swift movements he wrapped the end around itself, tugging down once more to finish. Then he held his hand out to her. "Let me help you on so we can adjust the stirrups."

Her first reaction was to refuse, but she realized how foolish that was. He was just being helpful. No reason to get all jittery about it.

In spite of her thoughts, as she dropped her hand in his she was far too aware of the roughness of the calluses on his palm, the warmth of his fingers as they clutched hers.

She settled into the saddle with a creak of sunwarmed leather and slipped her feet in the stirrups, lifting herself to gauge the clearance.

"How does that feel? Shorter? Longer?"

"It's good," she said, settling back against the cantle.

"Saddle sitting tight enough?" he asked, grabbing the saddle horn and pulling on it.

"Fine. Really."

"Just want to make sure you don't fall again," he said, smiling up at her, and for a moment, his concern created a delightful little tingle. It had been a long time since anyone besides her sisters had been this considerate.

"I think I'll be okay. I'm with you," she said, adding a saucy grin. "Super trainer."

"Just trainer," he said, untying the halter rope from the hitching rail and handing it up for her to tie around her saddle horn.

"What made you get into that line of work?" she asked. "Your father didn't do it, did he?"

"No. It was your dad, actually. And because it would take time to establish the business, he was also the one who encouraged me to become a deputy as a fallback."

Too many similar connections with her father, she reminded herself. Yet as he walked around Roany, talking to her, settling her down, Jodie saw the differences, as well.

Finn's patience. His quiet strength. He didn't need to use force to get his way. Just a quiet persistence.

Holding the reins, Finn rested his upper body on the saddle, as if to get Roany used to the weight, then put his foot in the stirrup, just standing there. Only when he sensed the mare wouldn't do anything unpredictable did he swing his other foot over the saddle. Roany sidestepped, but Finn drew her head to one side, making her go in a circle, like Jodie's father had taught her to do when a horse misbehaved.

Jodie's horse, Henry, stood stock-still, eyes closed, tail swishing at a few flies buzzing around them.

"Do you want to take the lead or shall I?" Finn asked, as he got Roany settled down.

"You go ahead," Jodie said, poking her toe in Henry's side.

Finn nudged the mare with his boots, turned her toward the trail and started her walking.

Henry followed, his head up high enough that Jodie knew he was paying attention, not so much that she worried he would try anything. She watched Finn ahead of her, moving in time with the horse's rhythm.

Despite the straw hat she wore and the time of day, the sun held enough strength to lay a blanket of warmth over her head and shoulders. The muffled thud of hooves hitting grassland and the occasional snort from Roany were the only sounds breaking the late afternoon quiet.

With each step closer to the trail and the pastures up in the mountains Jodie had spent so much time in, she felt the tension she had always felt on the ranch slowly loosen.

There was no one to disappoint, no one to be angry with her.

And as they rode into the cooling shade of the trees, she felt for the first time in years that peace was a possibility.

"It sure is beautiful up here," Finn said, pulling his horse to a stop on the rim of the valley overlooking the Saddlebank River below. From up here they could see the east part of town, the rest hidden by trees edging the pastures. "I think I can see my house."

Jodie chuckled. "Where is it?"

Finn moved closer, pointing with one gloved hand to an open area across the river. "See those buildings, the big white one in the middle of that large green space and the smaller one beside it? That's my place. Or will be when I save enough money to buy it."

"You live there now?"

"I'm renting it from Doc Wilkinson."

"Why don't you just buy it?"

"Vic always asks me the same question," Finn said, lowering his hand, fiddling with Roany's reins. "I have a timeline. In a couple of years I'll have enough for a comfortable down payment. I don't want to borrow too much." His plan always made perfect sense to him when he did his monthly accounting, but saying it out loud to someone like Jodie, it sounded boring and dull.

"But it might increase in value while you wait."

Finn laughed. "Again, you sound just like Vic."

"Sometimes you just have to jump in, I think. Go for broke."

"I've been broke," he said. "Don't want to be there again. Poverty can be scary."

"I thought your father had a steady job?" she asked.

"He did. But after he died, my mom managed to spend it all." The bitterness crept into his voice. "Sorry. You didn't need to know that."

"I always thought you had a good relationship with your mother."

"I think she tried. She was just…gone. Every time I thought I could count on her, she seemed to disappear. It got worse after my dad died."

"I remember my dad talking about you that summer, after your father died. He felt so bad for you."

"It was thanks to Keith that I got through all that. I was only fifteen and my mom was always gone. Always chasing after an elusive dream of doing more with her piano playing. She never seemed to give up on her idea of becoming a professional pianist, but it never came about. She had some opportunities and then…nothing. She would come home, stay awhile, then leave again. Your dad helped me out a lot during that time. He became a mentor to me."

Finn turned to Jodie, his voice growing sincere. "I want you to know how much I respected and appreciated what your father did for me. I was just a kid. Your dad would make sure I had enough to eat. He'd stop by after school to see if I was okay. I could have been put into a foster home, but I didn't want to go. I kept hoping my mom would come back. And she did, from time to time. But mostly, during those years, it was your dad who pulled me through. He was the one who brought me to the Moores' place once in a while, as well."

Finn gave Jodie a careful smile. "I thought I would let you know that your father was a good man."

She just nodded tightly. She seemed upset and he didn't know why. Did she miss her father more than she cared to admit?

"So what happened with the concert with Mandie?" she asked. "Why do you think your mother decided not to play?"

"Who knows? I've given up on trying to figure my mom out. I was thankful she arranged for Mandie to come sing at the festival. That was quite a coup. Apparently tickets are almost sold out, according to Amy." Finn turned to Jodie. "And that's why I'm glad you're playing."

"Even though you originally wanted my aunt," she said in a droll tone.

"I'm glad Laura suggested you," he insisted. "You've proved to be worth the trust she put in you." He glanced over at Jodie just as she looked at him.

She wore her hair loose today, and it flowed over her narrow shoulders like melted chocolate. She gave him a wry smile and for a moment he saw Keith McCauley looking back at him.

"You look just like your father," he said.

You're up on a mountain with a girl you're growing attracted to and that's what you come up with? He gave himself a mental smack on his forehead.

"Thanks. I think," she said, pushing her hair away from her face.

Unbidden came the memory of the moment in the corral the other day. That breathless feeling when he'd touched her. Part of Finn wanted to give in to the attraction he knew was growing between them, but that would be foolish. She was leaving soon, and in spite of that she wasn't the right woman for him.

Or so you keep saying.

He tried to banish the voice. Tried to be the practical guy he had always strived to be. He didn't want to end up on the wrong side of a broken heart again. He had a plan and he wasn't letting anyone or anything sabotage that.

"Your place looks nice from here," Jodie said.

"It's not as big as the Rocking M, your dad's spread, but it's respectable enough," Finn murmured, turning his attention back to the valley and his future.

"I always liked it up here." Jodie threaded Henry's reins through her fingers. "Whenever I found myself homesick, it was for this place rather than Knoxville."

"That's right. You do a lot of traveling."

"I do. I hope to do more once my sisters and I sell the ranch."

Her offhand comment brought reality crashing back to Finn. She wasn't sticking around. He needed to remind himself of that.

"Seems as though you've been everywhere."

"How do you know?"

"I heard about some of your trips from your dad."

Jodie released a harsh laugh, which puzzled him, and as if in reaction, Roany pulled her head back. Finn kept pressure on the reins until she stopped, then he eased off, praising her. She had been surprisingly well behaved, for which he was thankful. Getting her out on a ride was what she needed.

"So tell me about some of the places you've been," he said. "Sounds as if you've been all over world."

"You don't have a desire to travel?" Jodie asked.

"There are some places I'd like to see, but mostly I'm content here in Montana. It's home." His mom had traveled, but it hadn't made her any happier. "So what drives you to travel so much?"

"Get away. See something of the world. See other places and other cultures, but these days I feel like..." Her voice trailed off.

"Feel like what?" It was her melancholy tone that made him push her. As if her focus had shifted and he wanted to know to where.

She drew in a slow breath, absently stroking her horse's head, her movements slow and rhythmic.

"Like I'm not sure why I'm doing it anymore." She avoided Finn's eyes, her attention on Henry and the tangle of his mane. She fingered a few knots loose. "I feel as if I'm moving for the sake of movement. Trying something new. Trying to convince myself with all my flying around that I'm getting someplace. But lately, every time I arrive, I feel a sense of dissatisfaction. As if I still haven't found what I'm looking for."

Finn let her words settle in his soul, hearing the sorrow in her voice, the longing for something.

"'Our hearts are restless until they can find rest in You,'" he quoted.

She shot him a puzzled glance. "Who said that?"

"Saint Augustine. I read it one morning during my devotions. I often think of my mother when I hear it."

"She doesn't go to church, either?" Jodie asked, as if she included herself in that comment.

"Once in a while. When she feels she needs absolution."

"Does she find it in church?"

Finn wondered where that came from. "Do you?"

Jodie's expression grew hard and he wondered if he had overstepped. "I only went to church because it wouldn't do for the children of the sheriff of Saddlebank County not to attend."

"So it didn't mean anything to you?" The cynicism she was exhibiting bothered him. He remembered a young girl who would come to the youth group socials, laughing and singing exuberantly. Surely that hadn't been just for show?

"I wouldn't say that." She untangled another knot in Henry's mane, her movements slow and deliberate. "I always enjoyed attending the youth functions. I think… I feel like…God was more approachable there."

"So is God approachable to you now?"

She gathered up the reins, a signal to end the conversation. She paused and turned to Finn. "God and I haven't spent a lot of time together lately. I haven't exactly been…" She stopped there, shaking her head as if unwilling to say more.

Finn couldn't let that lie. He moved his horse right beside her, touching her arm, catching her attention. "God always seeks us, Jodie. Always."

He worried he might have been presumptuous, but she didn't move away from him. Finn shifted his hand to her shoulder, anchoring her, reassuring her.

As Jodie looked over the valley he felt her shoulders lower, as if she was letting herself take in what he was saying. "Being here makes me believe in Him," she said. "I feel peaceful here."

"God does reveal Himself in nature, as well as through His word."

Jodie's gaze drifted toward Finn, her expression puzzled now. "I never heard that before."

"It's what Vic's father used to say. Once in a while Vic, Dean and I would stay home from church, pack a lunch, saddle up the horses and go riding for the day. Vic's mom would be upset about it, but his dad said that there are times a man needs to see God's general revelation in nature. We would stop somewhere, eat our lunch, talk and pray."

"That sounds wonderful."

"It was. I was always so thankful for the Moore family," he said.

"You were fortunate to have them in your life. It sounds like their home was a haven for you."

Her choice of words made him wonder what her family life had been like, both here and in Knoxville.

"It was. They anchored me when my own life was so untethered. They showed me how family works."

Right now, he realized he had to remind himself what to look for in his own family. A Christian woman strong in her faith. A stable woman who valued home.

Denise had been that person for him, he thought. Then he glanced at Jodie, unable to deny the appeal she still held for him.

Was he being blind? Did his loneliness skew his perspective?

Did he dare risk his heart to find out?

Chapter Eight

Jodie sat down at the piano, spread the sheet music out in front of her and let the silence of the church surround her.

The building was empty. Yesterday, Sunday, it had been filled with people. In spite of her conversation with Finn up on the mountain on Saturday and his encouragement to attend church on Sunday, she'd stayed away.

Finn meant well, but she didn't need another reminder of how sinful she was. When she and her sisters had stayed at the ranch, church attendance had always been mandatory. As was the follow-up at the ranch, when their father went over the salient points of the sermon, hammering home to each of his girls the blackness of her heart and how she needed to repent.

Which only made Jodie all the more determined to show him *exactly* how black her heart was.

Closing her eyes, she banished the memories. Not for the first time she wished she could have confronted her father before he died. Asked him why he was so hard on her. She guessed some of it had to do with the day she'd seen her parents fight. Each summer she returned to Montana she had thrown that in his face, which made him angry with her, which made her rebel against him. But she also knew there was another reason he never saw fit to tell her.

Yet asking for that meeting was like wishing on rainbows, something she and her sisters often did when they were young. Wishing their mother was still alive. Wishing they could live together here on the Rocking M Ranch.

Later, wishing had turned into praying. Praying she could figure out what drove her and her father's off-kilter relationship. Praying she could understand him.

But it had all seemed futile.

She started playing, chasing away her memories with the sound of music. Mandie's first song was happy, cheerful and bright, and as Jodie played it, she smiled. She needed this happy song, this celebration of life. The verses spoke of a young girl playing in a sandbox, a mother with a baby, a man tossing a baseball with his son. A young couple drinking coffee. All connected by a chorus reminding people that our happiest moments could be found in our simplest enjoyments. It was a basic song filling a basic need.

Jodie ran through it a few times, finding her way through it, then set the piece aside and spread out the sheet music for the next one. She glanced over the words, then felt her heart slip. The song spoke of fitting in. Stumbling toward mercy and grace, making mistakes along the way, but always, always moving toward the offer of salvation.

The same things Finn had spoken of. The words that had created an ache and a yearning she couldn't rid herself of.

Jodie clenched her hands in her lap, tamping down her visceral reaction to the lyrics. She blamed it on Finn and how he had drawn out her confessions the other day. She hadn't intended to tell him any of that. It was as if, as she had accused him, he had been using the same patient tactics with her that he had with Roany.

And once again she wondered why he bothered. Why he cared what had happened that long-ago day. He had clearly moved on.

She pushed the thoughts aside. Telling him what she had was a mistake. Telling him more would only be a repeat of her conversations with her grandmother about staying away from the ranch, giving her sisters vague hints about the harshness of her father's discipline. They listened, but the skepticism on their faces showed they didn't believe her.

Finn had even less reason to believe, given his wonderful relationship with her father. She had to keep her distance from him.

Yet, as her fingers picked out the tune of the song, she felt again the warmth of Finn's hand on hers. How good it had felt to have someone offer her some connection. Some comfort.

She let the music wash over her, the mournful notes, the words about loss and seeking drawing out emotions she still struggled with. The loss of her dreams. The tangle of her life afterward. How she'd thought she had found a place with Lane, only to have him snatch it away.

She came to the chorus about God's grace offered free, but costing so much.

Her father always attached so many conditions on everything he did for them. Even the will, his last act, had been to bend them to his wishes.

Jodie let her hands continue to play, improvising now. She looked around the church, spotting the cross in the alcove at the front. Behind it were twenty-seven tiles up, twenty across, two of them water stained. When she was younger, she'd sat in their usual pew, counting tiles on the ceiling and the wall, the voice of the minister washing over her in an endless litany of words. Then as she got older, as she'd begun wondering how the world worked and why things happened the way they did, she began seeking. Actually listening at the youth meetings. It was there she'd discovered the notion of grace and forgiveness. Words she never heard at home.

Her hands slowed their playing as memories of those happier times brought up tears she had kept back for so long.

Was she crying?

Finn stood quietly at the back of the church, his eyes on the solitary figure playing the piano, her face raised to the ceiling, glistening tracks of moisture on her cheeks.

He recognized the song, one about loss and mistakes, and he wondered if Jodie was grieving some of the losses she had suffered. The losses she had revealed to him yesterday.

He exhaled, still trying to adjust his own thinking. He had to be careful. Jodie's life had too many red flags.

Her very presence at the piano was a reminder of the deal they had made. All part of her plan to leave.

And yet he couldn't eradicate that moment of connection they'd shared the other day. When he touched her, awareness hummed between them.

Finn straightened his shoulders and walked down the

aisle toward her. He knew the instant Jodie saw him. She stopped midbar, looked over at him, then turned back to the piano, wiping her cheeks with her hands.

"Sounds beautiful," he said, pulling out his measuring tape as he walked to the front. He had come to help Brooke Dillon plan the decorations for the concert. The fact that Brooke owned a hair salon seemed to qualify her, in Amy Bernstein's eyes, as someone well qualified to decorate.

"Thank you," Jodie replied, her voice echoing in the cavernous space.

When he went to church yesterday, he had half hoped she would be there, too, but he hadn't seen her. He wasn't sure why that bothered him.

"Has Brooke come yet?" he asked.

"I saw her briefly at the Grill and Chill before I came here. She was talking to George."

"I thought she didn't want to see him again." Brooke's crush on George Bamford was no secret, but last Finn had heard, she'd declared she was over him.

Not so much.

"They seemed quite animated and Brooke seemed pretty happy." Jodie shuffled the sheet music and looked as if she was about to get up.

"Don't leave on account of me," Finn said.

"If Brooke is coming, I should go."

"No. Stay. She's just coming to talk decorations with me. I like hearing you play. You've got such a gift for it."

Jodie flushed at his praise, then with a shrug set out the music again, ran through a couple scales and started playing the next song. This one was more lively, a version of a popular worship song. Finn remembered his mother playing it in what she called her "religious" stage.

Finn had liked that stage. She had been more peaceful, more at ease with herself. Less absent and isolated. Of course, it hadn't lasted long, and soon she was heading to other places, chasing her elusive dream.

He watched Jodie play, watched her fall into the music. He drifted closer, drawn by the smile on her face.

"I like the words of this one," he said, coming to stand beside her.

"I've never heard it before." Jodie hit a wrong note, then stopped.

She looked up at him, their eyes meeting, awareness once again arcing between them.

"You're making me nervous," she whispered, starting to play once more.

His breath caught in his chest as he thought of that moment they had shared on Saturday up on the mountain. He knew he should move away from her. But he couldn't forget the sorrow he had just seen on her face, the unspoken pain he had heard in her voice the other day.

He sat on the bench beside her, the melody pulling out better memories, and before he realized what he was doing, he was picking out an alternate tune on the higher keys with his right hand, flowing into what she played.

Without missing a beat, she shifted her own hands down an octave, maintaining the rhythm. The music wove in and out, each of them improvising as they went.

Finn felt the tightness in his chest loosen. A loneliness that had been his steady companion since Denise died eased away.

He pushed aside the constant analyzing and let the music flow. Let himself enjoy being with this very talented woman.

They came to the end of the song. Jodie added a few bars to finish it off, then lowered her hands as the last notes faded into silence.

They sat a moment, joined by the experience.

"You play better than I expected," she finally said, her genuine smile bringing out his own.

"I think that's a compliment."

"Sorry. I'll amend that. You play very well."

"Not as good as my mother, but I can hold my own. She taught me until I got into my too-cool-to-play-piano stage and stopped."

Jodie laughed as she went to gather the papers, just as he was about to do the same. The sheets of music spilled onto the steps of the stage the piano sat on. Finn jumped off the bench, bending over to grab them at the same time she did, and their heads cracked together.

Jodie sucked in a pained breath and Finn's forehead throbbed. They both sat back on the steps looking at each other with a dazed expression.

"That was awkward," she said with a nervous laugh.

Then Finn noticed a trickle of blood running down her temple. "You're hurt," he said, catching her by her arms, steadying her.

"I think I just broke open the cut I got when Roany dumped me," she said, touching her forehead.

He caught her hands. "Just leave it. Do you have any tissues?"

"In my purse. Beside the bench."

He grabbed her purse and handed it to her. She pulled

out a package of tissues and fumbled with it, the blood now dripping down her cheek.

He tugged the package from her hands, yanked out a tissue and pressed it against her head. "I'll go get a cloth from the kitchen," he said.

"No. It's okay. Don't bother."

He hesitated, but the blood flow was easing up. He pulled another tissue free and, brushing her hands aside, gently dabbed at the cut. "That should probably have had a stitch or two," he murmured, leaning closer to look.

"I've had worse."

She spoke quietly, their faces now inches away from each other. He felt his breath quicken when her thickly lashed eyelids lowered, then lifted again.

His breath stilled and it was as if time itself slowed.

He rested his hand on her shoulder, his other still holding the tissue to her forehead. As he suppressed the voices warning him to be careful, to watch what he was doing, he lowered his head to hers.

Jodie moved closer at the same time, their lips meeting halfway.

Finn slipped his hands around her back, nestling her against him. He pressed a kiss to her cheek, to her other temple, then rested his chin on his hair. Cradling her against his shoulder, he let out his breath in a sigh that released all the stress of the past few months.

This felt right. This felt good.

That warning voice in the back of his head reminded him she was leaving. That he didn't need this complication in his life.

That he couldn't trust his emotions.

He kissed her again, stilling the voice. Allowing himself this moment with her.

Chapter Nine

Jodie closed her eyes, her arms wrapped around Finn, his strength and support a brief moment of refuge.

How long had it been since she could let someone else be strong for her?

All these years she'd been running around, trying to find what she had found here.

She drew in a deep breath, as if centering herself, finding her balance in this new place.

Finn brushed his hand over her hair, his movements soothing.

She didn't want this moment to end. As soon as she pulled away, life would come crashing back, and with it, the reality of their situation. She and Lauren were selling the ranch and she was leaving.

Why?

The single word spiraled up through her objections and plans.

She lifted her head, looking into Finn's eyes as if trying to find a reason there.

He smiled at her, tucking a strand of hair behind her

ear, and started to say something when a voice broke into the moment.

"Finn Hicks. Are you here?"

Brooke Dillon. Jodie pulled back, shifting sideways on the stage away from Finn, hurriedly looking around for something to do. She saw the papers still lying on the steps beside her and gathered them up, her hands shaking.

She should have left ten minutes ago. She didn't want to see Brooke, or anyone else, for that matter. Not so soon after kissing Finn.

"At the front of the church," he called out.

Finn got up, reaching out to help her to her feet, but Jodie didn't dare touch him. She didn't trust her own feelings right now. She clutched her papers and stood on her own.

"There you are." Brooke hurried up the aisle. The young woman's cheeks were flushed and a bobby pin clung to the end of a blond curl that Jodie suspected was supposed to be anchored to her head. This was a sharp contrast to the fitted blazer and white shirt she wore over tailored slacks.

From the way Brooke's eyes glowed as she got closer, and the faint smear of her red lipstick, Jodie guessed she wasn't the only one dallying.

"Sorry I'm late," Brooke said breathlessly, pushing back the wayward curl. "I was just at the Grill and Chill. Talking to George." She stopped, her eyes flicking from Finn to Jodie. "I hope I wasn't interrupting anything?"

Jodie flushed and kept her attention on the sheet music she was straightening. She wanted to leave now. Other than her brief glimpse of Brooke at the diner, the last time she had spoken with her was two weeks after she'd missed her date with Finn and her audition. A couple days before she'd had to leave for Knoxville. Jodie had been hanging out with Jaden at the gazebo in Mercy Park. Brooke had come along and they had poked fun at her, teasing her about her unrequited crush on some young man whom Jodie couldn't even remember. Jodie knew she had been horrible and had tried to find Brooke to apologize, but Brooke and her family had left town for their summer vacation.

Though she wasn't the type to hold grudges, she would surely remember Jodie's behavior that awful summer.

"Not at all," Finn said, plucking a stray bobby pin out of Brooke's hair. "Not the best advertisement for a hairdresser," he teased as he handed it to her. "So what were you up to at the Grill and Chill?"

Best defense is a good offense, Jodie thought, unable to hide her smile at Finn's deflection.

"Well…I just…" She paused, then shook her finger at him. "None of your business."

"But I'm guessing it was George's?"

"This has nothing to do with George," she said, though from what Jodie had heard it had everything to do with him. She turned to her. "Hello, Jodie. How are you doing?"

"I'm okay."

"I was sorry to hear about your father. He was a good man."

"So I understand."

Brooke's eyes narrowed and Jodie sensed she'd said the wrong thing.

"I know he was sorry he didn't see much of you," Brooke added. Jodie wasn't sure she imagined the imperceptible censure in her voice. Looked as if most of the people of Saddlebank were on her father's side.

Thankfully, Brooke turned back to Finn. "And I'm sure today isn't easy for you, either."

He looked puzzled.

"It's been four years ago today," Brooke continued. "Since Denise passed away."

Ah, yes, thought Jodie. *The perfect fiancée.*

"Right," said Finn, shooting an awkward glance at her. "I forgot."

"I'm surprised you did," Brooke said, laying a gentle hand on his shoulder. "I know you miss her so much." Then she lowered her voice, but not low enough. "Be careful, okay?"

Jodie's cheeks flushed again at the implied warning in Brooke's voice. Was there anyone in this town on her side? Anyone willing to give her a second chance?

She hurriedly shoved the sheet music inside its envelope, all the while fighting down the unwelcome feeling of shame bubbling up in her.

I'm not a horrible person, she wanted to shout.

But she kept her thoughts to herself. She didn't know Denise, but it didn't matter. Whatever and whoever she was, Jodie was fairly sure Denise had been a much better person than Jodie had ever been. After all, according to Finn, she was the kind of girl her father had wholeheartedly approved of. Unlike his own daughter.

"I should go," Jodie said, tucking the music under her arm while avoiding Finn's eyes. "Nice seeing you again, Brooke," she said.

"I'll be by the ranch again tomorrow," Finn called out.

She tossed him a wave over her shoulder as she practically ran out of the church, wondering why she'd ever agreed to this.

But even as she drove away, memories of Finn's kiss lingered.

And what was she supposed to do about that?

Finn parked his truck at the corrals of the Rocking M. He pushed his hair back from his face. It had been a long day. It was as if all the troublemakers and psychopaths had got together and decided that today was Crazy Day.

He had one character cooling his heels in the county jail after Finn found him brandishing a gun, threatening his ex-girlfriend. After he'd tackled the guy, he'd discovered it was a fake firearm.

Then some fool had crashed his car into an abutment of the bridge over the Saddlebank River. His blood alcohol level had been over the legal limit, so he'd joined the first guy in the jail.

Which meant Finn had spent most of his afternoon getting statements and filling out paperwork. Something he was behind in from yesterday because he'd had to meet Brooke at the church.

The only thing that had got him through the day was the thought of seeing Jodie again.

He recalled once again the kiss they had shared yesterday. From a practical viewpoint it hadn't been the smartest thing.

So why did it feel right?

Finn thought of that moment in church when Brooke had expressed her sympathies. He had forgotten about the anniversary of Denise's death. Every year since she died, he'd put flowers on her grave. In fact, at Keith's funeral, when he'd stopped by Denise's grave site, he had been trying to decide what flowers he would bring this year.

But he'd forgotten. This year he'd been distracted by a pair of haunting blue eyes.

He laid his head back on his vehicle's headrest, closing his eyes as he prayed. *Lord, I'm confused here and I'm scared I'm making a bad choice. Help me to keep my focus on what's important.*

He waited, as if letting the prayer soak into his heart, as well as his soul. Reminding himself to be objective and in charge, he got out of the truck, pulled in a deep breath and tried to calm himself.

The door of the house opened and his erratic heart skipped a beat.

Jodie walked toward him, her hair shining in the afternoon sun. She was wearing an orange tank top, her hands shoved into the pockets of a pair of baggy purple pants that would look more at home in a harem than on a ranch.

As she got closer, his initial eagerness was tempered by the frown on her face. The way her steps slowed as she came nearer.

"Hey there," he said with false enthusiasm. "I noticed you've got Spot and Roany penned up."

She nodded, tossing her hair back. "You don't have to do this, you know. Work with my horses. And if you can find someone else to play…" She waved her hands as if erasing what she had just said. "I know we had a deal, but I can't… I'm not…" Her voice faltered, then he caught the faintest quiver of her lip.

"Jodie, what's going on?"

She clenched her jaw and tightened her hands into fists. "I'm sorry," she said, turning away from him.

His concern morphed into confusion and he caught her by the arm. "There's something you're not telling me."

She kept her eyes averted, straining to pull away. "This is a bad idea. You shouldn't be with me."

He kept his hand on her arm as he struggled to catch up. "What are you talking about?"

This time Jodie managed to pull free. "We kissed each other. It's probably best to move on from that. Act as though it didn't happen."

Though he had been thinking the same thing only a few moments ago, hearing her say it out loud made him upset.

"I don't know about you, but I'll have a hard time forgetting about that," he said, forcing himself to remain calm. "And from the way you reacted, I think you will, too."

Jodie shook her head. "Don't do this."

"Do what?" he asked, sensing her weakness. He took a step closer, her nearness making him throw aside any caution he might have had. He cupped her face, turning it toward him. "Don't look at you? Don't let myself enjoy being around you?" He felt her resistance melting, saw it in the flare of hope in her eyes.

He capitalized on that, his other hand resting on her shoulder, a gentle invitation to stay near.

"I heard what Brooke said about being careful, and she's right," Jodie said, looking away. "From what you said about Denise, I know she was a good person. I'm not that person."

Finn had to admit that he still had misgivings about

Jodie. But standing in front of her now, feeling the way he did, all those misgivings seemed petty and unimportant.

"You don't have to be that person," he said, stroking her cheek with his thumb, turning her face up to his, the reality of her easing away memories of Denise. "You just have to be you."

"That might not be enough."

"You're a good person regardless of how you like to come across. And I'm not sure what to do about what's happening with us, but I feel as though I'd be a fool not to see where it might lead this time."

Her shoulder lowered and her hand caught his wrist. Her fingers were icy cold but her cheek felt warm.

"What if it doesn't go anywhere?" she asked. "Then what?"

Finn didn't know the answer to that, and truth to tell, with her looking up at him with those incredibly blue eyes, he didn't want to think any further than this moment.

"Let's just take it one step at a time," he said. He bent his head and touched his lips to hers. She curled her hand around his neck, her fingers tangling in his hair as she responded to his kiss.

He pulled away and smiled, pleased to see her smiling back at him.

"You're making me even more confused," she said, breathless.

"I'm sorry. I didn't mean to do that. I just feel as if our story isn't finished yet."

Her hand stroked his cheek. "Then, we'll just have to see where it goes."

"Would you be willing to go to lunch with me on

Friday? I'm working night shift tomorrow and Thursday, otherwise we'd do it sooner."

"Are you asking me out on a date?" Jodie teased, lowering her hand, but resting it on his chest.

"If you have to ask—"

"Yes. Yes, I'm willing. Anytime I don't have to sit at home eating grilled-cheese sandwiches is a good day."

"And no television, either, I imagine."

Jodie gave him a look of mock horror. "Something as wasteful as television? In Keith McCauley's house? Surely you jest."

"Well, I'm not jesting about the work we need to get done today," he said.

"Of course. We don't want to waste time now," she said with a wink, then spun around, walking ahead of him, her hair swaying, a bounce in her step.

He laughed at her comment, but heard beneath that an edge he couldn't define. The more time he spent with Jodie, the more he found out about Keith, and Finn didn't know what to do with the information.

Maybe he was too concerned with having everything just right.

Maybe he should allow himself this moment. See where it went.

And stifling any second thoughts, he followed Jodie to the horses.

Chapter Ten

Friday afternoon Jodie pulled into an empty spot in the shade of a maple tree and looked out over Mercy Park, its gazebo sheltered from the midmorning sun by the cluster of ash trees.

A vague memory surfaced. Of her father, getting her to smell her ice cream, then tapping the bottom of the cone. Her nose had hit the ice cream and they all laughed. Then he'd pulled a hanky out of his pocket, wiped her nose and gave her a big smile.

She let the memory settle like a warm blanket over the colder, harsher ones. This, too, was part of her past with her father.

She got out of her car, locked its doors, then laughed at herself. In a town like Saddlebank, it was hardly at risk of being stolen, but she didn't want to take the chance. This car was her way out of here.

Or was it?

What should happen when she left Saddlebank?

Would she be staying in Wichita? Moving on? Waiting for the ranch to sell so she could finance another trip abroad?

She couldn't work up any enthusiasm for the ideas. However, the thought of meeting Finn at the Grill and Chill did. Was she being smart about this? Did she dare?

Ignoring the endless questions swirling in her head, she smoothed her hands over the bright blue silk tunic she had bought in a bazaar in Bangkok, paired with blue jeans she had put on for her date. Trying to straddle the line between her identity and what she thought it should be?

Maybe she should have worn the baggy pants she had picked up in Thailand. Just to remind herself who she was.

As she stepped up onto the sidewalk, someone called her name. She turned around to see Aunt Laura walking toward her, arms outstretched, her poufy gray hair tossed about by the spring breeze.

"Hello, my dear girl," her aunt called out. "I haven't seen you for ages," she chided. "What are you doing in town?"

"Sorry, Aunt Laura, I've been lying low at the ranch," Jodie said, returning her tight hug, but not directly answering her question. She pulled back, smiling at the faded ring of lipstick on her aunt's mouth, the smudge of mascara around her eyes, her eye shadow gathered in the creases of her eyelids. Aunt Laura always managed to look vaguely put together, but not quite hitting all the marks.

"Doing what?"

"Helping Finn with the horses. Getting stuff sorted in Dad's office."

Aunt Laura made a face. "That will be a job and a half. That man was turning into a pack rat."

"There's enough paper there, that's for sure." Jodie

hadn't even begun to get it all sorted out. "I hope to have it filed and organized before Lauren comes. And deal with the horses, too."

"Speaking of horses, how is the arrangement with Finn going?" Laura asked, giving her a broad grin.

"It's coming," Jodie said, ignoring the speculation in her aunt's eyes. "I think Finn has Roany behaving how he wants her, and now he's working with Spot."

"So do you know when you'll be selling them?"

Jodie was taken aback momentarily at her aunt's question, then reminded herself that was the purpose for Finn training the horses. "I'm not sure. I have to talk to him about that."

The thought of selling them depressed her.

You could keep them.

Where? And for what?

A few people passed them, murmuring a quick hello. Laura returned their greeting, then turned back to Jodie. "I hear Mandie is coming on Wednesday," she said, shifting her focus. "That's exciting. I imagine you're looking forward to practicing with her. You always did like a challenge."

"I hope that I'll be able to meet her expectations."

"You'll do fine," Aunt Laura said, patting her on the shoulder. "You're a gifted pianist."

"Not according to Amy Bernstein. She thinks I'm unreliable."

"Well, to be honest, honey, you've had your moments."

Jodie looked past her aunt toward the park, recalling the variety of memories it had evoked. "I was a different person then."

"An angry young girl." Laura hooked her arm

through Jodie's, pulling her close in a half hug. "And you had your reasons. I know my brother, and while he wasn't the greatest father, I would like to say he tried his best. But after your mother—" Aunt Laura stopped there, shaking her head. "Sorry."

"After my mother what?" Jodie pressed.

"Where are you headed?" her aunt said, changing the subject. "I doubt you came into town simply to chat with me."

Guilt suffused Jodie. "I'm going to the Grill and Chill."

"Who are you meeting there?"

Jodie didn't want to tell her, but knew she was postponing the inevitable. Aunt Laura's connections in Saddlebank were vast and varied. It would only be a matter of minutes after she sat down with Finn that her aunt would find out. "Finn. We have to make some plans."

"Plans? Really?"

"About the horses," Jodie said with a note of finality.

"Of course." Aunt Laura's eyes sparkled as she grinned up at her. "I'm headed in that direction. I'll walk with you."

She caught Jodie by the arm again, nodding a greeting at two other women whom Jodie vaguely recognized, then waving at a man who beeped his horn at them.

Small towns, Jodie mused, walking along with her aunt. Part of her had missed these connections. This feeling of being grounded.

You could stay.

The thought tantalized. But what would she do here? How would she make a living? Jodie had no answers to that.

"Well, here you are," Aunt Laura said, stopping at the entrance of the diner. "I'm meeting Sylvia and Annette at the quilt shop. We're making a new quilt for the craft fair coming up this summer."

"Sounds like fun."

Her aunt kissed her on the cheek. "Say hello to Finn for me?"

Jodie nodded, said goodbye and stepped inside the diner, where the noise of people chatting washed over her. She had arranged to meet Finn at about one thirty, hoping to miss the noon rush, but the diner didn't look any emptier than it had when she and Lauren met here after their father's funeral.

She stood by the front counter, looking around. She saw a few familiar faces in the crowd. Two older women, Alice Fortier and Ellen Bannister, sat by a window with a younger one with long brown hair. Jodie recognized her as Keira, Ellen's daughter and a distant relative of hers. Obviously pregnant, Keira shifted, pressing her hand to her stomach. She glanced up, looking puzzled when she saw Jodie, as if trying to place her, then smiled and waved her over.

Jodie checked behind her, just to make sure she was looking at her.

"Hey, Jodie, how are you doing?" Keira asked, clumsily getting to her feet as Jodie approached the table. She gave her a quick hug. "Sorry I didn't make the funeral. I was feeling kind of rotten that day."

Truth to tell, Jodie didn't remember her absence, but Keira seemed genuinely sorry, so she just smiled and said it was okay.

"Do you want to join us?" Keira was asking.

"Thanks, but I'm meeting someone."

"You'll have to come up to Refuge Ranch sometime," Ellen chimed in. "I was sad I missed Erin. I haven't seen her for ages, and though I enjoyed catching up with Lauren, we didn't have enough time."

Lauren and Erin had hung around with Keira and her sister, Heather, whenever they came to town for their summer visits. Jodie, ever the rebel, had preferred the company of Jaden and his crew whenever Clair had decided she didn't want to hang out.

"Lauren is coming back here in a couple of weeks."

"Tell her to call me. Heather would love to see her, too."

"I'll do that." Jodie wondered when it would be polite to walk away from them. Then Finn suddenly materialized beside her, smelling like soap and outdoors and…Finn.

He greeted everyone, made the appropriate amount of small talk, then, with a hand at the small of Jodie's back, guided her toward an empty booth at the rear of the diner.

Jodie settled in, unable to stop the fluttering of her heart when Finn sat across from her, his smile resulting in the most attractive crinkles at the corners of his hazel eyes.

"How was your shift?" she asked.

"Quiet, thankfully. Just a couple of speeding tickets and one disorderly conduct. Piece of cake," he said with another grin.

"Speeding. Who would commit such a nefarious deed?" she asked with mock horror as she picked up the menu.

"There are a lot of heavy-footed drivers in Saddlebank County. I've nabbed more than my fair share."

"Serve and protect," she quipped.

"Actually, our motto is Protection with Honor."

"I know. I heard it many times," she stated.

"Of course you would, though I'm having a hard time imagining your dad working it into ordinary conversation."

"Not much of that happened in our house." Even as she let the words slip, the ice-cream memory returned and with it a few others of sitting in this very diner, having supper. Joking, laughing. And then her aunt's vague comment about her mother came to mind.

"You're frowning again," Finn said, reaching across and taking Jodie's hand. "What are you thinking about?"

"My aunt said something about my mother. But she never finished the statement." Jodie looked up at Finn, curious now. "Did my dad ever talk about my mom to you?"

He shook his head. "Not that I can think of. Just that he was divorced and she passed away four years later. Why?"

Jodie shrugged. "Just wondering. I'll have to quiz Aunt Laura later." She didn't know if it would help. But what her aunt had said made her dig deeper into her own past. Wondering what that initial fight between her parents had been about.

"And what do you think you'll have to eat?" Finn asked, changing the subject. "Not that the menu has changed much over time."

"My aunt and my sister always tell me I pick unhealthy stuff, so this time I'm going with soup and salad," Jodie said, glancing over the laminated menu. "What does George have for the soup of the day?"

"It's Friday, so I'm guessing clam chowder," Finn

said. "And the salad would be spinach avocado with feta cheese."

"The fact that you know the menu so well makes me think you eat here too often," Jodie said. "Don't you have a kitchen at your place?"

"It's not my place yet, but yeah, I do."

"Do you ever use said kitchen?"

Finn gave her a warm smile that made her curl her toes. "Why don't you come over on Sunday after church and see for yourself?"

Church followed by lunch at Finn's place?

Jodie hesitated, wondering if she was ready to do that. Practicing the piano at church the other day had been enough. Actually attending? Being reminded of how sinful she was? Did she want to put herself through that?

"I'd like to see your place. Could I meet you there instead? At about noon?"

Finn's smile dimmed just enough to make her realize he was disappointed.

She wanted to explain, but wasn't ready to expose herself like that. People in Saddlebank had long memories, and an out-of-control sheriff's daughter had raised a lot of eyebrows, brewed a lot of gossip.

Brooke's words still whispered through her consciousness.

Be careful.

Jodie would do well to heed that warning.

Finn wasn't going to be discouraged by Jodie's reluctance to go to church. One step at a time, he reminded himself, as he looked back down at the menu in front of him.

Besides, he wasn't sure himself how this would end. *Then, what are you doing all his for?*

Because, deep down, he clung to the hope that Jodie was still the girl he had at one time been attracted to. Not the girl he had seen hanging around with Jaden Woytuk the rest of the summer, driving like a maniac, flouting the rules and partying.

Something besides her getting grounded that summer had happened somewhere along the way, and Finn was sure if he found out what, he would have a better understanding of who Jodie was now.

"Are you ready to order?" Allison, George's sister and full-time waitress, arrived at their table.

"I think I'm going with a burger and fries," Finn said, setting the menu aside.

"Great. Now I'll be suffering food envy." Jodie scrunched up her nose, which made Finn smile. "But I'm going to be strong and stick to my guns, mix my metaphors and hold the course. The main course that is. I'll have the soup-and-salad special."

Allison chuckled, then left, taking their menus.

Jodie leaned forward, one of her dangling earrings catching on her hair.

"Where did you get those?" he asked, reaching across to untangle it.

"Some hard bargaining with a young man in a bazaar in Jordan." Jodie flushed as Finn took the opportunity to gently touch her cheek, then pulled his hand back.

"What was in Jordan?"

"I went to see the lost city of Petra. Check out Aaron's tomb. Biblical dude. Moses's brother and spokesman."

"You know your Bible."

"I know my Bible characters," she corrected.

He wondered why she sounded so defensive.

"So what was it like? Jordan?"

"Hot. Challenging. Interesting. I like how traveling broadens my thinking. Helps my perspective."

"Where would you go next?" He asked the question casually, as if it didn't matter, when he was surprised how much it did. Her plans for another trip meant she would leave. And he didn't like to think about that.

Jodie fiddled with her earring, flipping it around as she considered his question. "I don't know."

Her response kindled a flash of hope.

She gave him a faint smile, then shrugged. "But that's a conversation for another time. Tell me about your place. How did you find it? What do you plan to do with it?"

"Do you have a couple of days?"

She laughed, resting her elbows on the table, looking genuinely interested. "Tell me."

"I'm renting it right now. As for what I plan to do with it, I think I'll save that for when you come over to visit."

She looked as if she was about to say more when Finn heard someone calling his name.

Brooke came walking toward them carrying a stack of papers. "Do you have a minute?" she asked, looking at Jodie, then him.

He was about to say no, but didn't have a chance. Brooke just barreled on.

"I'm so stuck," she said. "I was supposed to make decorations for the church festival, but Anita ducked out on me. I can't find anyone to help. Abby is busy taking pictures. Keira, whom I can usually count on, is too pregnant. Heather is gone all next week." She pushed her hair back with one hand. "Do you know anyone?"

Finn looked at Jodie, disappointed that Brooke didn't even glance her way. Brooke was one of the kindest people he knew and probably didn't intentionally freeze her out. But he saw from the way Jodie looked down that she might have felt the unintended slight.

"What about you, Jodie? Would you be willing to help?" he asked.

"She probably doesn't have the time," Brooke protested.

"Actually, I do have time," Jodie said, surprising him and Brooke, too, judging from the way her eyes widened. "What do you need help with?"

"Um, well…are you sure?" she stammered.

"Yes. Just give me a glue gun or sewing machine. I'm sure I can't mess it up too badly." Jodie's smile seemed false, and as Finn glanced from the one woman to the other, he felt a tension between them. He had noticed the same awkwardness when Brooke had come to the church. At that time he had chalked it up to the kiss he and Jodie had just shared.

But now he wasn't sure. It seemed as if something else was going on.

"Okay. I guess that could work. Can you come Monday?"

"Sounds good."

"Will you need me?" Finn asked.

"Not until we're ready to set up, which I wanted to do on Thursday, the day before the actual concert." Brooke turned her attention back to him, but Finn could tell by the way she wrinkled her nose that she was uncomfortable.

"I'll need to check my schedule, but I should be able to make it." This concert cut deeply into his horse training time, but, he had to admit, so did spending time with Jodie. And training her horses didn't get him any income, either.

But as he glanced over at her, he knew it was well worth it.

"I'll leave you two alone, then," Brooke said, clutching her papers to her chest, her expression confused as she looked over at Jodie. Then she left.

Finn watched her leave, surprised to see George standing outside the kitchen, doing the same. He retreated back to his domain, whistling.

"Looks as if things are on again between those two lovebirds," Finn said, turning back to Jodie. But she wasn't looking at him; she was looking out the window, following Brooke's progress down the street. "So how do you and Brooke know each other? You didn't go to school here."

"I saw her off and on over the summers. She was friends with Keira, and Keira would hang out with Lauren and Erin." He saw a glimpse of sorrow in Jodie's face. "Part of a past I don't want to talk about," she said.

The determined tone of her voice told him he wasn't getting any more out of her. He also knew he didn't have the right to push for more information.

But if she kept all these secrets, how was he to get to know her better? How were they supposed to get anywhere in this relationship?

And could he even call what they had now a relationship?

Chapter Eleven

"So here's my share, tip included," Jodie said, pushing some bills across the table.

Finn looked at her as if she had given him something contagious. Then he shoved the money away. "Take this back right now," he said with a note of disgust.

Jodie laughed as she pushed it back at him. "Seriously. I want to pay my share."

"I'm sure you do, but I don't want you to." He ignored it, got up and walked to the front counter before she could say anything more.

She grinned, pocketed some of the bills and left a few behind for her own tip. She'd worked as a waitress enough to appreciate how welcome a good tip was. She suspected Finn would tip as well, so Allison would be well paid by them.

She joined him at the counter while George rang up their order. The tall, lanky man was smiling, another surprise. He used to run the diner with his father, and Jodie remembered a sulky twenty-year-old who looked as if he wanted to be anywhere else but in Saddlebank.

She had always identified with him.

"Have a fantastic evening," George chirped as they left. "Thanks for choosing the Grill and Chill."

Clearly he was in a good mood, and Jodie wondered if it had anything to do with Brooke's visit.

While they were inside the diner, the sun had dipped below the mountains and dusk had fallen over the town. The streetlights were beginning to glimmer on. Jodie felt a sense of settling down, as if pulling a blanket around oneself, getting ready for the evening.

"Do you want to go for a walk?" she asked. "Down to the river? I haven't been there in ages."

"That'd be great. Hopefully I won't have to bust up a party there," Finn said.

Jodie caught his grin, but behind that came a surge of shame at the thought of all the parties she'd attended farther down the path.

They walked past her car to the end of the street, then turned left toward the river. The street curved, and soon they arrived at the walking trail the Chamber of Commerce had set up in a bid to get more tourists to Saddlebank.

Jodie lifted her face to the sky, letting the cool breeze coming off the water wash over her.

"Did you miss this place? When you were away?" Finn asked.

She glanced sidelong at him, then nodded. "Knoxville was home, in a way, but my first recollections are of the ranch and this town." She laughed. "In fact, when I stopped by Mercy Park, I had a good memory of me and my family. Eating ice cream there with my mom and dad. Laughing."

"Just one memory?"

The question in his voice bothered her. "For now."

"Was it that hard? Coming here every year?"

"I guess every year I hoped it would be different, but it wasn't. In fact, the last few years it was harder than ever. I know I wasn't the best daughter, but it's hard to build a relationship when you are constantly being told what a horrible person you are." Jodie's voice faltered and Finn slipped his arm around her.

She wanted to pull away. Everything she said broke down another bit of Finn's esteem of her father.

"Was it always bad? Your relationship with him?"

She sensed another underlying question in his voice.

Was he truly that bad or is it just your skewed idea of the relationship?

Jodie held Finn's gaze and tried to see the situation through his eyes. Party girl who was out and about every night. Solid, dependable man who was part of the community. A sheriff who was good at his job.

Doubt shimmered in the back of her mind and she tamped down the temptation to tell Finn everything. She doubted he would believe her and she couldn't stand to see that on his face.

"Anyway, that was a good memory."

"I'm glad you're remembering some good ones," he said.

"Maybe after two months here I might remember more."

"Or make a few more," Finn said.

She gave him a sidelong glance, disconcerted to see him looking at her, his expression intent. She felt hope and possibilities building up in her chest.

"Always good to have those."

They walked along in silence, Finn's presence comforting and appealing at the same time. Then, after a few moments, he stopped. She turned toward him, anticipation thrumming through her.

"I don't think I told you how beautiful you look today," he said, stroking her hair away from her cheek, fingering her earring.

Jodie couldn't stop the blush warming her face. "Can't hear that too much, I guess."

"I could say it again, if you want."

She just smiled, knowing that asking would make her seem vain.

"I know there's something else I'd like to say again." He paused a moment. "Come to church with me."

"Church? I don't know…" In spite of her hesitation, she held the idea, testing it.

"I know you used to go," he continued. "I'm sure that something, in all those years, stuck. Some glimmer of God and of how He sees you?"

"Well, that's part of the problem. I'm not sure how God sees me." *God and the rest of Saddlebank*, she thought, remembering how Amy Bernstein had spoken to her.

"Come and find out," Finn urged. "At least come and sing some songs. I know you love music."

This meant a lot to him. Finally, she conceded. "Okay. I can do that."

Finn wrapped both his arms around her. "Great. And then lunch at my place."

Her heart fluttered at the thought. Suddenly things seemed to be moving quickly. She was just catching her balance in this new place she had come to.

But as she looked up at him, saw the hope in his expression, she knew her attending church was important to him. Right now, she didn't want any more barriers to their relationship.

She grew still, her heart slowing.

Was that what was happening? Did she dare think that far?

Then Finn stroked her hair, as if easing away her questions.

She had to let go for now, she reminded herself. Just take it one step at a time.

"Sure, I'll come to church and then to your place," she said. "How could I miss out on the chance to have a deputy sheriff cook for me?"

"Cook might be a stretch. But I know how to handle a frying pan."

Jodie laughed and nodded. "This I've got to see," she said.

"I look forward to amazing you."

Then, to her surprise and pleasure, he bent and brushed a sweet, gentle kiss over her lips.

She felt her heart quicken, but then a tiny whisper of concern flitted through her mind.

Be careful. You don't know what lies ahead.

Finn stood in the foyer of the church, his anticipation growing as the doors opened, then sinking again when a husband, wife and two children entered. The clock over the elevator told him that in two minutes he would have to go into the service by himself.

He checked his disappointment. He had been so sure she would show up. Though he knew it would be difficult for her, he had hoped Jodie would come to church anyway and find some comfort.

And maybe, just maybe, she could find her way to forgiving her father.

The door opened and this time he saw the silhouette of a young woman, but it was only Brooke. She gave him a brief greeting, hurrying past him to the stairs leading to the basement, carrying a large plastic tub full of colorful paper. He guessed she was teaching Sunday school to the youngsters this morning.

When he heard the singing group starting up, he knew it was time to go. He pushed down his own disappointment, trying to be understanding. He had time, he reminded himself. Jodie wasn't leaving for at least another month or so.

The thought made his stomach churn. They weren't there yet, and if he were honest with himself, he still had some concerns. But for now, he was willing to see where things went.

Just before he turned to walk into the sanctuary, he saw a head of dark hair, a flash of purple, and then there she was.

"Hey there," he said, happiness suffusing him when Jodie walked up to him.

She wore her hair loose, flowing over the shoulders of a bright purple sleeveless dress shot through with shining threads. Over her shoulders she had thrown a gauzy scarf edged with silver. Hoops hung from her ears, matching the silver shoes she wore.

She looked exotic and beautiful.

"I like your dress."

"Mumbai," she whispered, glancing nervously around the now empty foyer. "Am I too late?"

"Just on time," Finn said, offering his arm.

She took it, smiling, and together they walked up the stairs and into the church sanctuary.

The usher led them to an empty spot, and as Finn stood aside for Jodie to enter, he saw her falter. He glanced down the pew, wondering what had made her hesitate.

Amy Bernstein was looking at them, her brow furrowed.

Finn remembered what Jodie had told him about her relationship with Amy and her daughter.

But there was nothing he could do now. He glanced over at Jodie, who to his surprise lifted her head and gave Amy a cool smile. The woman's frown deepened and she looked away.

Finn noticed the flush on Jodie's cheeks, and he prayed that Amy's seeming disapproval didn't take away from the service for her.

Then he looked over at Jodie and felt it again. That peculiar connection holding her to him. He knew on one level he had to be careful, but he couldn't deny how he felt about her.

Then the singing group started a new song, encouraging everyone to stand and join them.

As they did, Jodie leaned over to whisper in Finn's ear. "Can't believe my aunt is okay with drums and guitars in church."

Finn caught her hand and gave it a gentle squeeze. "Your aunt is cooler than you realize."

"Clearly," Jodie said, adding a grin. Then she joined in the singing, her voice tentative at first, but then as she caught the tune, clear and melodious.

Finn watched her, hope whispering in his heart.

They sat down and the pastor invited them to open their Bibles to Psalm 32.

"'Therefore let all the faithful pray to You while You may be found, surely the rising of the mighty waters will not reach them. You are my hiding place, You will protect me from trouble…'" These words were familiar to Finn. He'd clung to them when he was alone, waiting yet again for his mother to come home. Words he'd wrapped himself in after Denise's death. He prayed regularly that God would be his hiding place and protection.

Because the reality was his mother was never around. Always gone. And Keith had become his protection.

Finn wondered if Jodie would ever understand what his life had been like. In spite of the difficulties she'd had, there had always been someone around for her. Either her grandmother or her father.

It wasn't until Keith had come into his life that Finn had felt the same sense of being taken care of that he had before his father died.

As he glanced at Jodie, he prayed that she, too, would come to know that the Lord's unfailing love would surround her, as well. That she could think of positive things about her father.

Then he felt her slip her hand into his and he squeezed lightly.

She was here, with him, in church.

It was a start. He just had to pray that she wouldn't hurt him.

Because the reality was he was growing more and more attached to her. The idea both excited and frightened him at the same time.

She had let him down once before, had let her father down.

Would she do it again?

Chapter Twelve

All the way from church to Finn's place, Jodie couldn't get the pastor's message out of her mind.

The peace and protection that God offered. The opportunity to start over. The pastor spoke of God's love as being unconditional. This was a surprise to her.

Her father had preached about a God who required much and was satisfied only when people were obedient.

Jodie had a hard time melding the two visions of God in her mind, and yet as the pastor spoke she'd felt a softening of her soul. She felt the possibility of a relationship with the God that Pastor Dykstra seemed to know.

She followed Finn's truck as he turned down a tree-lined drive that curved, then opened up into a large open space.

Jodie parked her car and got out, feeling a sense of homecoming as she looked around.

The place Finn called home seemed to welcome her in a way her father's ranch never had. A small log house was tucked against a grouping of trees, and peonies filled the flower beds flanking the porch, sending their spicy fragrance over the yard. The sidewalk leading up to the house was made of rich red paving stones framed with green moss.

This place felt like home.

Finn walked over to her, smiling with pleasure, seemingly happy she was here.

"So. What do you think?" he asked, pride in his voice.

"It's beautiful," she said as he joined her. "I can't believe you haven't already bought it."

"I will. Once I have enough money."

"How much is enough?" Jodie asked.

"Well, to quote J. D. Rockefeller, 'just a little bit more,'" Finn said. "I don't want to end up being mortgage poor. Living hand-to-mouth."

"Did you have this place when you were engaged to Denise?"

"I did, but we had a plan. We were both going to save up until I could put enough money down so that our debt load wouldn't be too high."

"I wouldn't wait too long." Jodie looked around the yard again, letting the peace and hominess fill her. "Someone else might come and snatch this place up while you're lining up your waterfowl."

"Maybe," Finn said. "I want to make sure that I don't extend myself too far. Don't want to take unnecessary chances. I've lived enough with that kind of mess. I have to be responsible."

"Always good things to be, but sometimes you have to go for the things you want," Jodie said, giving him a quick smile. "Take a risk."

He bent over and kissed her. "I'm not much of a risk taker."

"You took a risk sitting with me in church," Jodie said, forcing a laugh to cover the frustration she felt thinking of Amy sitting down the pew from her, emitting waves of disapproval.

"I made a choice to sit with you in church," Finn said, his voice serious.

Jodie's thoughts ticked back to the hugs she'd gotten from Keira, Heather and their mother after the service. The smiles from Monty and the welcome she got from Alan, the local mechanic she saw whenever she had to bring her dad's truck in.

But she didn't imagine the surprised looks she saw on other faces or the condemnation on Amy's. Whenever thoughts of staying in Montana strayed into Jodie's mind, it was the unspoken censure of some of the townspeople that seemed to counterbalance the others.

"Do you want to see the rest of the place?" Finn asked, inclining his head to the yard beyond the house.

She heard the pride in his voice and nodded. "I'd love to."

He took her by the hand, and like two schoolkids they walked through an opening in the trees. "That's the riding arena I fixed up last year." Finn pointed out a large barn painted red. Two sliding doors were open, giving Jodie a glimpse inside. Metal panels were stacked along one wall and straw bales beyond that.

It was connected to a fenced-in paddock, and beside that lay the round pen. Everything was excruciatingly neat and tidy and well kept.

As they neared the paddock Jodie heard a whinny and saw out in the pasture a group of horses, heads up, watching them.

"Are those yours?" She walked toward the wooden

rail fence, watching as the boldest one warily approached this stranger to her domain. Jodie guessed the leader was a female. They usually were.

"The palomino is a potential barrel racer I'm training for a woman in Great Falls. Heather Bannister—sorry, Heather Argall—has been helping me train the horse. The bay is mine. Buffy. She's one of my broodmares. Purebred quarter horse. Her first colt is the one right beside her. Her second colt is likely out in the field yet."

"So how many horses do you have?"

"I've got fifteen of my own and six that I'm working on for other people."

"No wonder you wouldn't take mine," Jodie said, leaning on the fence, reaching out to Buffy, who cautiously approached them. "How do you find the time to work with them, do your farrier work and keep Saddlebank safe?"

"I do what I can when I can. And lately, well, there's this girl that's been a major distraction to me."

Jodie felt the tickle of a blade of grass on her cheek and slanted Finn a grin. "You should learn to apply yourself."

He ran the grass down her cheek again, then turned to his horse, which was now nudging his shoulder. "Personal space, Buffy," he warned, lifting a hand.

The mare stopped, then took a step back. Finn waited a moment, then made a kissing sound and Buffy moved cautiously toward him.

"Good girl," he murmured, stroking her head.

"You're always training them, aren't you?" Jodie asked.

"Always."

"It's the deputy in you, I think," she said with a light

laugh. "You like law and order, which you then apply to your horse training."

"Or it could be the horse trainer in me that likes law and order, which translates well into being a deputy."

Buffy's colt joined them at the fence and Jodie stroked her nose, tickling it with her fingers to see if she would lift her lip.

"Do you like it? Being a deputy?" she asked. Even though her father didn't have to work—he could have lived off the ranch if he'd managed it himself—he'd spent more of his days in his sheriff's car than on a horse. Whenever he got ready for a shift, he'd looked eager to go as he strapped on his belt, checked his pistol. Every time he did, it was as if he transformed in front of her.

"I do. But for me it's a means to an end. This is where I want to be."

Jodie felt another small resistance to Finn ease away. And behind it, an equal note of panic.

Spending time with him, being around him, was getting too easy. He was taking up a space in her heart she had told herself was closed for good. Lane's disbelief in her had hurt more than she cared to admit. It was too similar to her father's. She wasn't sure she wanted to make herself that vulnerable ever again.

"My dad would be disappointed to hear that," she said. "He lived to be a sheriff. I'm sure quitting the force was hard for him."

"I think he felt as though he'd lost his purpose when that happened." Finn took her hand, tracing the scar on the back, his expression serious.

Jodie had to fight her impulse to pull her arm back.

"You always have this bitter edge in your voice when

you talk about your father." Finn spoke quietly, but she sensed an indistinct edge to his voice. "He might not have been the best person, and I don't know precisely what happened between you two, but he often lamented the fact that you didn't speak to him or come to visit. I know it hurt him, but maybe forgiving him would help."

The words were almost laughable. There was no vague interpretation of what her father had done to her. He'd hit her. Often.

But how could she tell Finn? Would he believe her?

Jodie remembered the first time her father had struck her. Her sisters were visiting their cousins at the Bannister ranch. Keith had come home from work grumpy, tired. It had been a bad day. She had made a smart remark to him when he'd asked her why supper wasn't ready.

He had swung around, fury in his eyes, and struck her on the shoulder.

Her sisters had questioned her version of events, as did her aunt when Jodie tried to tell her. When she'd tried to tell them a second time and they still hadn't believe her, she was so angry she'd known she needn't bother again.

And then there was Lane.

Too easily she recalled the look of condescension on his face when she'd tried to explain to him what had really happened. Not only did he not believe her, he then piled pain on top of disbelief. He'd told her that it was time they broke up. That she wasn't the person he was looking for. That she wasn't good enough.

She couldn't bear it if Finn were to have the same reaction.

She glanced down at her hand. The scar that she looked at every time she played piano was barely visible now, but it was still a reminder of the secret attached to it.

"Have you forgiven your mother?" Jodie seemed to throw the words at him, daring him to pick them up.

Finn's expression didn't change. Instead, he shrugged. "I've had to find ways to forgive my mother each time she comes back into my life. It may take some time, but I have to let go of my bitterness or it will take over."

His words underlined what the pastor had preached about this morning when he'd talked about the bonds of bitterness and how they could cling and dominate one's life. How God offered freedom from those bonds.

"I'll think about it," she said.

"And I'll be praying for you," Finn murmured. Then he frowned at her. "Why are you smiling?"

She caught the hurt in his voice. "I'm not laughing at you. I'm just thinking how nice it is to be in someone's prayers. That hasn't happened for a long time."

"I think your father prayed for you," Finn suggested.

Jodie heard the unspoken plea in his voice and behind that the affection he held for her father. It created a disconnect she couldn't acknowledge.

"That's nice to know," she managed to answer.

For now she had to leave it be. She wasn't sure where she and Finn were going, though that thought held less uncertainty each moment she spent with him. He was becoming important to her and was making her think of changing her plans.

Finn opened the door of the house and Jodie stepped inside, her eyes adjusting from the bright spring sun to the darker interior.

Homey was the first word that came to mind. Homey and masculine and incredibly tidy. To her left, heavy leather couches flanked a stone fireplace, fleece-lined throws lying neatly folded over their backs. To her right lay the kitchen, with wooden cupboards and granite countertops, a gleaming sink and taps. A large island with a butcher-block top. A set of knives sitting precisely beside a cutting board.

A bay window in the dining room overlooked a small pond, the rustic table and chairs in front of it appearing handmade.

"Don't tell me that, on top of deputying and training and tidying, you also make chairs?" she teased as she walked over to them, running her finger over their backs.

"No. I bought those at a fund-raiser the church held last fall. Dean, Vic's little brother, made them. He's a carpenter and making chairs was a type of therapy for him after his rodeo accident."

"Is Dean the person the minister prayed for this morning?"

"Yes. He's been struggling. Trying to move on from the past."

"Aren't we all?"

"You thinking about the pastor's sermon?" Finn asked, unerringly catching what she meant.

She hesitated, not sure how to articulate her scattered thoughts. His comments reminded her of other times when she was in church, when she could feel a hint of God's presence. Like an echo of a piece of music she could barely hear.

"I like how he said that every day was new and

fresh," she said. "An opportunity to start over. How God comes to us each day with the same patient offer."

Come to Me all you who labor and I will give you rest.

The words had resonated in her mind. Whenever she had been in church with her father, his presence had loomed so large that it had become hard to hear the invitation she had heard this morning.

Returning here to Saddlebank felt like a step backward. Back to a time she had been outrunning.

And yet sitting in church today, she'd heard once again that gentle encouragement. Maybe because her father wasn't sitting beside her—a constant reminder of how unworthy she was to respond to that gentle call.

"I'm glad you came," Finn said, staying where he was by the dining room table.

"I'm glad, too," she said. "I felt as if I was being offered something I need."

"And what is that?" he asked.

"Acceptance. Rest."

The puzzlement on his face showed that he would like to hear more, but she didn't know if she was ready to talk about her desire to be someone else. She wasn't sure what shape that should take.

Instead, she walked over to the fireplace and the mantel with pictures arranged on it. Jodie recognized Finn's mother in the first one. Christie Hicks stood in a field of flowers, her hair loose, her bright dress swirling away from her in a blur of color as she spun around, head lifted to the sky. She looked like a throwback to the sixties. "When was this one taken?" Jodie asked, tilting it toward Finn.

"About six years ago. She had been doing well that year."

Jodie heard the sorrow in his voice and turned back to him. "We talked about my father yesterday, but I'm sure you had your own struggles with your mother."

Finn nodded, his arms crossed over his chest, his feet planted apart. Like a deputy.

"The hardest part of dealing with my mother was feeling as though I didn't matter to her. I know much of her difficulties had to do with my father's death." He gave Jodie a rueful smile that looked much like the one on Christie's face in the picture. "She wasn't dependable, and that's hard when you're the only one in the house."

Beside the picture of his mother was a studio photo of a young woman, blonde, beautiful and slender, smiling at the camera, poised and elegant.

"Is this Denise?" Jodie asked, lifting it to look closer. The woman's blue eyes gazing back at her seemed kind and gentle.

"Yes it is." Finn's voice held a note of reverence, and Jodie could see why as she looked at the next image. Denise smiling an infectious smile, wearing scrubs, leaning close to a young boy in a hospital bed. The child's head was tilted toward her, his hand clutched hers, hope in his expression. "You said she was a nurse?" Jodie asked.

"She was in her last year of training when...when she died."

The little boy looked as though he would walk through fire for the woman standing beside him.

Jodie glanced at the next picture. Denise in the hospital again, holding a baby, looking maternal and gentle.

Tough competition, Jodie thought.

She shook it off, but as she turned back to Finn, she wondered if he compared her to Denise.

"She seemed like a good person."

"I am thankful she was in my life." Then he smiled at her. "Just like, right now, I'm thankful to have you here."

The light in his eyes and the grin on his well-shaped mouth were both encouraging and inviting. So she stood on her tiptoes and brushed a kiss over his mouth, as if claiming him. Reminding herself that she was here with Finn. Not Denise.

"So you ready for me to make you something to eat?" he asked.

Jodie felt a gentle settling in her soul. "Yes. I am."

"Then, sit down and observe a master at work," he said, pulling out a loaf of bread. "You need to know that I make the best grilled-cheese sandwiches this side of Saddlebank."

"Put a pickle with it and I will acknowledge your culinary mastery," she teased.

Finn laughed, buttering the bread. As he got cheese out of the fridge, Jodie couldn't help glancing once more at the pictures on the mantel. Denise seemed to be looking at her. Judging her.

I fall short, Jodie thought. *But I'm trying.*

And that was all she could do.

"I like this color," Brooke said, fingering a swatch of gauzy material etched with swirls of pastel pink and blue and green. "What do you think?"

Like an Easter egg, Jodie wanted to say, but wasn't sure that Brooke had taken her along for her artistic input.

"The colors are lovely," she prevaricated.

Brooke frowned at the vague comment. "I'm guessing you don't like?"

"I like it, but I'm thinking of what Mandie's music is like. A bit edgy, avant garde and yet approachable. I think you might want to emphasize that concept."

Brooke bit her lower lip, destroying what was left of her pink lipstick. "What did you have in mind?"

"What do you think of sticking with a basic white-and-black concept?" Jodie suggested.

"Sounds stark."

"Yes, but if we use lots of sheer white material for a backdrop, add some black accents, either musical notes or musical scores, then use some of those black metal stands you showed me to hold vases of bright red roses, all of varying heights, I think it could look dramatic and elegant at the same time."

Brooke was still frowning and Jodie immediately regretted giving her input. "I'm no decorator..."

"But you have a unique sense of style," Brooke said wistfully. "You always did. I mean, look at you now."

Jodie glanced down at what she wore. A simple shift over leggings, belted with a scarf, a cluster of cheap gold chains around her neck. "This is nothing special. Found this at a bazaar in Bangladesh, and the pants are from a thrift store."

"You do have a knack for pulling it all together and standing out. Always did. Even when you and your sisters were younger and were here in the summers."

"Again, thrift store."

"Your dad was that broke?"

"No, my mom was that broke. My dad never let us go shopping here. The only time we went to town was when he took us to church or we went to stay at friends'. Approved friends. The Bannisters and you for my sisters, Clair for me. He was pretty strict with us."

And before she could see more denial of her father's personality on Brooke's face, Jodie moved over to another display, fingering the bolts of material, wishing she hadn't gotten pulled down this memory lane. She was tired of feeling as if she might have imagined everything her dad had done to her.

"What do you think of this?" she said, pulling out of the bargain bin a bolt of cloth that had a faint silvery sheen to it. "It's cheap enough that we could use lots of it and fill the front of the church."

"I like that a lot," Brooke said as she pulled some off to see how it draped. "Let's take it. Now I need a few things to make centerpieces to put on the hors d'oeuvres tables after the performance. There's a craft section on the other side of the store."

They poked around, looking for items, laughing about some of the more outrageous ideas they came up with.

"This is like planning a wedding," Jodie declared as they chose candleholders and runners, trying to bring the white, black and red theme into the centerpieces.

"It is, isn't it?" Brooke said. "The last time I did this was with Denise…" She stopped herself, looking agitated. "Sorry. Didn't mean to bring her up."

"She was your friend?" Jodie asked, unable to stifle her own curiosity about the woman who once held Finn's heart.

"She was a real sweetheart."

"So I understand."

Brooke gave a wistful smile. "I was so happy for

Finn when he started dating her. His own mother was so undependable. As you well know. That's the reason you're playing at the festival instead of her. But Denise. She was a rock for Finn. Someone he could rely on. Such a strong Christian and just what he needed."

Each word Brooke spoke hooked like a barb in Jodie's soul. She sensed Brooke was simply being honest, but as she talked, Jodie knew she was more like Finn's mother in personality and behavior than like Denise.

And the thought hurt more than she wanted to admit.

"And it's been four years since Denise died?" Jodie asked.

"Four years ago on the day I met you and Finn at the church," Brooke said, setting everything on the counter. "I can't believe he forgot. He goes every year to put flowers on her grave."

Jodie thought of Finn's visit to a grave the day of her father's funeral. Initially she had thought it was his dad's, but now realized it must have been Denise's.

The salesclerk rang up the purchases and Brooke pulled her purse off her shoulder to pay, then let out an exclamation. "Oh, no. I left my wallet at home. Stupid me." She turned to Jodie with an apologetic smile. "Do you mind paying? I'll reimburse you as soon as possible."

Jodie glanced at the total and did a mental calculation of her own funds. She had paid a few bills yesterday that might not have gone through yet.

She would have enough to cover this, she told herself.

She swiped her card through, then felt her heart sink as the word *denied* popped up.

"Try again," she told the clerk. "I might have punched in my PIN wrong."

But once again that heart-sinking word flashed on the screen.

Of course this had to happen in front of Brooke, friend of Denise, who probably never had a bank card declined.

"Sorry," Jodie said to Brooke. "I can't cover this."

"What are we going to do? I don't have time to come running back here again," she whined, rubbing her finger alongside her nose as Jodie slipped the useless bank card back in her purse, trying to think what she would do herself. Yes, she had some money in her savings account, but she would run out of that before she finished her two-month stint here.

Once again the irresponsibility of her lifestyle hit her hard. Once again she heard her father yelling at her to set money aside for a rainy day, whatever that meant.

Brooke rummaged through her purse again and then with a triumphant cry pulled a credit card from its depths. "I'm so sorry. I forgot I left this in here last time I used it," she said. "I'm so scatterbrained."

Jodie smothered a flush of resentment as the other woman paid for the purchases. If it wasn't for the flush that stained Brooke's cheeks, Jodie might have thought her act was deliberate.

They walked out of the store and it wasn't until they got into Brooke's car that she turned to her. "I'm so sorry," Brooke said, sounding genuinely apologetic. "I didn't mean to put you on the spot like that."

"It's fine. I thought I had enough in my account. I'll just need to make a transfer." Jodie needed to talk to Drake, her father's lawyer. He had mentioned funds she could access.

"But still. I hate it when something like that happens to me. I feel so useless. So irresponsible. It's so embarrassing."

Please stop reminding me, Jodie mentally pleaded. "I guess we're even now," she said, giving Brooke a pallid smile.

"What do you mean?" Brooke looked genuinely puzzled as she started up the car.

"That summer. Before I left?"

She frowned. "No. Sorry, I still don't know what you're talking about."

"You don't remember me and Jaden Woytuk sitting in the gazebo when you walked by? We said some unkind things."

Brooke slowly shook her head, as if trying to dredge up the memory. Jodie could tell the moment the quarter dropped, as her dad liked to say.

A pained shadow flitted over the woman's features and she looked ahead, her hands tight on the steering wheel.

"You remember now, don't you?" Jodie said, her voice subdued.

Brooke nodded and pulled into the traffic flow.

"I'm so sorry," Jodie said, doubting that Denise had ever done anything so unkind. "I wasn't a good person back then."

Brooke gave her a vague smile, then turned her attention back to her driving. "It was a rough year for you," she said. "I heard about you skipping the audition. I'm sure you had your reasons. Every time I saw your father at the café, he mentioned it. Said how bad he felt for you."

Jodie pressed her lips together, fighting down the

urge to set the record straight. "So why did you tell Finn to be careful?" she asked.

Brooke pulled in a slow breath, as if considering her next comment. "It was legitimate, I guess. I knew Finn was attracted to you once before. You're still kind of fun and interesting, like you were when you and your sisters came to visit. I also know that after Denise died, he fell into a deep funk. I just wanted him to make sure he wasn't moving too quickly with you. I didn't know you would be sticking around."

Jodie felt like she should be insulted, but instead found herself envious of Finn and the community around him. People who cared what happened to him.

How long had it been since she'd felt that? Had she ever? Bouncing back and forth between Knoxville and here hadn't ever given her a sense of continuity in her life.

And now? She could be a part of this if she made smart choices now.

"I don't want to interfere." Brooke was quiet a moment, then laughed, giving a self-conscious shrug. "Who am I kidding? Of course I want to interfere. I like Finn. And I haven't seem him smiling like this in a long time." She grew serious. "But I think it's only fair to let you know that Finn is a straight shooter. His mother disappointed him so many times. I still remember his face whenever his baseball team would play and his mother promised to show up and didn't. It happened to him so many times it was heartbreaking."

"What are you trying to say?"

Brooke tapped her fingers on the steering wheel, then shot Jodie an apologetic look. "I know your past and how hard it must have been, getting shunted between here and your grandmother's home in Knoxville. But the reality is you do have a bad reputation here. I know Amy wasn't crazy about you playing for Mandie, and she's been trying to find someone else, but you're here and Finn's mother isn't. I just hope that…that…"

"I don't let Finn down."

"Kind of, yeah."

Her words were probably not meant to hurt, but they did. Jodie thought of Amy and the disapproval that emanated from her like a wave. It seemed she wasn't keeping her opinions to herself.

Jodie hid her pain, turning to watch the landscape flow past as they headed back to Saddlebank.

Bad reputation.

She knew it herself, but hearing it from Brooke created another stream of questions.

Should she encourage Finn at all? Was she wasting her time and his?

Yet despite her concerns, she felt a rightness with Finn she had never felt with Lane, or any other man. For the first time in years, as they drove back to Saddlebank, she had a sense of heading home.

Could she do this? Hadn't she always promised herself she would remain true to who she was?

And yet, as she thought of Brooke's comment about Finn's happiness, vaguely attributing that to her, Jodie felt a peace she hadn't experienced in a long while.

If she had to change to make Finn happy, she could do that. Couldn't she?

Chapter Thirteen

Finn yanked open the door of the church, glancing at his watch as he did. He had promised Donnelly he would cover the night shift again, but he wasn't due back at work for another hour. He knew Mandie was coming today to run through the music with Jodie, and he wanted to make sure everything was okay.

Had nothing to do with possibly seeing Jodie again, he told himself, yet his heart jumped at the thought.

Silly and scary how that woman could do this to him. A few weeks ago he had a plan in place for his life, and now he was thinking of ditching it. Going for broke, as Jodie had teased him about.

He had talked to Dr. Wilkinson, the owner of the ranch he rented, and to his surprise the doctor had been encouraging. Thankful, even, that Finn had finally made a decision. Apparently his hesitation had made Wilkinson wonder if Finn was still interested in purchasing the property.

Now things were shifting and he was stepping into unfamiliar territory. Was Jodie part of this?

The thought made Finn anxious. He was being cautious, but he had a right to be.

He heard the sound of a piano, a voice speaking over the music and he hurried his steps. Jodie was here already and, from the sounds of other voices talking he heard, Mandie, as well.

When he stepped into the sanctuary, Finn immediately looked for Jodie. But he didn't recognize the person sitting at the piano. Hair pulled back in a severe ponytail. White shirt. Black slacks.

Mandie stood on the stage, holding a microphone, consulting with a man who wore a headset. Her sound guy?

Finn glanced around the church and his heart sank. Amy sat in the front row, turned back to chat with a couple other strangers seated behind her. Probably more of Mandie's crew, Finn thought. Laura, Jodie's aunt, sat a few seats back.

But there was no sign of Jodie.

Had she bailed on him? And if she had, who was at the piano?

Then Mandie walked over to the pianist and talked quietly to her. The woman nodded, then glanced over her shoulder as Mandie walked back to her sound person. Finn stopped in his tracks.

The stranger at the piano was Jodie?

Why was she dressed this way? Had Mandie asked her to change her style of clothing?

He wandered into the sanctuary, feeling off-kilter at the sight of Jodie looking so…conservative.

She wasn't even wearing earrings.

Then she saw him and her smile and wave settled

his concerns. Just Jodie being Jodie, he thought, making his way up the aisle.

"How is it going?" he asked as she got off the bench and came to join him.

Her smile shifted, looked more forced as she glanced past him to where Amy sat. "Mandie just needs to check the sound. But we're making headway."

That seemed an odd way to put it.

Then Mandie came back again and Finn turned to her, holding out his hand. "Good afternoon. I'm Finn Hicks."

"Ah. Then, I would suppose that Christie is your mother?"

"Yes. I'm sorry she couldn't be here."

"I am, too." The performer gave him a tense smile, then shot a quick glance Jodie's way.

"Is everything okay?" Finn asked.

"Everything is fine. No problem." But the hasty way she spoke and her artificial humor made him think there was, indeed, a problem. Mandie gave Jodie a nod. "Shall we try it again? From the top of the second song. And I'd like to see if we can't inject some life into the piece?"

Jodie looked Amy's way, sat down at the piano again and, on Mandie's count, started playing. She fumbled the first few chords, found her way back and then abruptly stopped. "Can we try again?"

Mandie didn't even look at her, just nodded.

Finn heard Amy's heavy sigh as she got up. If he were honest, he'd admit to feeling nervous himself. He stepped back, wondering if his presence wasn't making Jodie anxious.

"Finn. Can we talk?"

Amy stood beside him, tapping his arm to get his attention.

Laura looked over at them, her expression concerned, but she stayed where she was as Finn and Amy walked to the back of the sanctuary.

"I have to tell you that I'm worried about Jodie playing this Friday," Amy was saying. "I know we're pressed for time, but I think we need to find somebody else."

As they spoke, Jodie started playing again, but her accompaniment sounded stilted compared to how he knew she could perform. He tamped down his own second thoughts. Jodie was just nervous. That was all.

"Were you thinking of asking Laura McCauley?" Was that why Jodie's aunt was here?

Amy waved off that suggestion. "No. Not at all. She's just being a lookie-loo."

"I though Jodie was doing fine?"

"Mandie Parker is not the kind of person you play 'fine' for," Amy said, making little quotes with her manicured fingers. "She needs excellent. Is there any way, any way at all, you could contact your mother?"

Finn thought of the endless text messages he had sent his mom before Jodie showed up, the vague replies and then the silence that was typical of communications with his mother. "No. I don't think I can."

He didn't want to go through that humiliation again, trying to reach out to a woman who contacted him only when it was convenient for her. He had spent too much of his life hoping she would come. Hoping she could put him first. He wasn't doing that again.

"I don't think she's a better player," Finn said, feeling a bit disloyal. "And in spite of how you think Jodie is doing, I know I can count on her."

"I still don't like this," Amy said.

"Well, at the moment, unfortunately, we don't have any other option."

That didn't come out right, but before he could correct his words, Mandie was talking. "Okay. I think we need another break," she called out.

"I better go see if she needs anything," Amy said, sounding self-important. She strode down the aisle, arms swinging, as if headed into battle.

Finn joined Jodie at the bench. She was paging nervously through the music, as if trying to find a different order to the notes.

"Hey. How's it going?" he asked, as he sat down beside her, though he could tell from the lines around her mouth and the way her eyes skittered to the front that it wasn't going well.

"I don't know. Hard to find the right balance," she said. She looked up at him, her expression uncertain. "Maybe I shouldn't be doing this. Maybe your mother should be playing."

Was Amy putting ideas in her head? Or was it the other way around?

He cupped Jodie's shoulder, tightening his grip, disappointed at her attitude. "I heard you play the other night. You *should* be doing this. You are an amazing pianist and I'm not one to hand out compliments easily. Just relax and be yourself. I believe in you."

She looked up at him and her smile made him feel better. He bent down and brushed a gentle kiss over her lips. But as he drew away, he still saw uncertainty in her eyes.

"You can do this," Finn said. "I know you can."

"How do you like my outfit?" she asked.

Her question was as unusual as it was unexpected. He glanced at her plain clothes, knowing he was heading into murky waters. Was she looking for a compliment? That was so unlike her.

"Elegant," he answered. It was all he could muster.

She gazed down at her pants, smoothing them with her hand. "That's what I was going for." Then she gave him a beatific smile and he felt he was back on solid ground.

"I thought I would stop by before I went on my shift. And to let you know that I won't be around the next few days. I just got a call from the lady up in Great Falls I'm training those horses for. She wants me to deliver the gelding to her and help her out the first day he's at her place."

"Really?"

The disappointment in that single word ignited hope in him that Jodie would miss him. He was just overly sensitive to her moods. Things were growing more serious between them and every moment they spent together took him a few steps closer to a place he'd never thought he would be again.

Making plans around a woman. Letting old dreams resurrect.

"I'm sorry. I have to go."

"Of course. This is all part of you building up your business."

"You gonna miss me?" He couldn't resist asking that.

"I will," she said, reaching up to stroke his chin.

"I'll miss you, too." He gave her another kiss, and then Mandie was calling her, telling her which piece she wanted to do.

"Sorry. I've gotta get back to work," Jodie said. "Have fun with the horse."

"It will be a riot." He gave her hand an encouraging squeeze. "See you in a couple of days. And don't worry about your playing. Just be yourself. That's all you can be."

"I wish I could be better than that," she replied obliquely.

But before he could quiz her about it, she gave him another smile, then turned back to the piano. Mandie was at her mic again and giving Jodie the cue to start.

Finn hesitated, wishing he could pinpoint exactly what seemed off as Jodie played. He had heard her that night when they'd played together. Heard the emotion that ignited the song, brought it alive. He had felt as if the music was a living, breathing thing, filling up the auditorium and his soul.

Now, she sounded as if someone had deflated her. Technically she played well, but the spark seemed to be gone.

He wished he could stick around, give her more support. But since making the deal with Dr. Wilkinson, Finn needed the money he would get from his client for part of his down payment. To collect it, he had to deliver the horse.

He lingered another moment, then sent up a brief prayer. *Be with her, Lord. Watch over her.*

Finn sensed she would need his prayers, because something was going on and he couldn't figure out what.

He walked across the parking lot toward his truck just as a woman got out of a small red car—a car like the one his dad used to own.

She wore her graying hair in a long braid down the back of a white shirt worn loose over a pair of flowing white pants.

His footsteps faltered as he belatedly recognized his mother. She'd worn her hair loose the last time he saw her, and her face had looked less drawn.

But what was she doing here now? Especially after she'd said she wouldn't be able to play?

He walked toward her, frustration and disappointment mingling with a feeling of hope. The same emotions he always felt each time he saw her, each time she sent him an email or text message.

"Hello, Mother," he said as she came toward him, her smile hesitant.

"Finn. So good to see you." She held her arms up to give him a hug.

He stepped forward and returned her embrace, then pulled back.

"Sheriff Donnelly told me you'd be here," she said, scratching her arm with her fingers. "I was hoping to connect with you."

"It's good to see you," Finn replied.

"I wanted to see you. I just want to say I'm sorry—"

"How have you been?" he asked, cutting off the automatic apology she gave him every time she saw him.

He knew he should be warmer. Kinder. But disappointment after disappointment with her made him wary.

Her eyes locked on to his, her expression yearning. "I don't know what else to say but that I'm sorry."

He gave her a strained smile as he acknowledged her apology.

Forgive me, Lord, he prayed, knowing he wasn't

playing his part as the loving and forgiving son. *She has let me down so many times.*

And the fact that Jodie was now practicing in the church auditorium was physical proof of that. The fact that it all turned out well was a blessing in spite of his mother, not because of her.

"So it seems as if you managed to find a suitable replacement for me," she said, waving one hand toward the church. The sounds of Jodie's playing floated out an open window over the parking lot.

"Yes. Jodie McCauley. She's very accomplished."

Just then a discordant note sounded and Finn tried not to wince.

"I heard that from Mandie," his mother said.

Finn narrowed his eyes as her words registered. "Did Mandie call you?" he asked, unable to keep the defensive note out of his voice. "Is that why you've come? To take over from Jodie?"

He knew she wasn't playing to her full potential, but surely—

"No. No. Not at all." His mother fluttered her hands in protest. "I haven't spoken to Mandie since…since I told you I couldn't play." She pressed her lips together as she hugged herself. "I'm sorry I put you in a bind." She stopped there, as if sensing her apology wouldn't be welcome. "I just wanted to make sure things worked out for you."

Finn tried not to look at his watch. To acknowledge the ticking of the clock. He still had to go home and load up the horse, then head out. The sooner he could leave, the sooner he could return and support Jodie. He sensed she could use all the help he could give her.

"Things worked out quite well after all." He returned

his mother's smile, feeling he was short-changing Jodie by using the word *well*. "Fantastic, in fact," he amended. "And now I have to apologize. I'd like to stay and chat, but I have to leave for Great Falls to deliver a horse, and unfortunately, I won't be back for a day or two."

"Of course. You're a busy man."

Her words were like a small reprimand, but she could hardly hold him to account when she had been the one to jump in and out of his own life. She could hardly expect that he would be waiting for her reappearance.

"Will you be coming to the concert?" he asked.

"I'm not sure—"

"You should. I'd love to see you there."

She seemed to consider his request, then nodded. "I think I might. I'd like to see Mandie again. And I'd like to hear Jodie play."

Finn glanced over his shoulder at the church, listening. Jodie was playing the piece again. It sounded better, but he knew she wasn't performing at her full potential.

"She'll be great," he told his mother, praying it would be so. "I hope to see you there." Then he took a reluctant step back, feeling as if he was abandoning Jodie and his mother both, and feeling more guilty about the former than the latter. "I have to go. I'll see you when I get back."

Then, sending up a prayer for forgiveness, and support for Jodie, Finn got into his truck and drove away.

"Can we run through that one more time?" Mandie called out from her position behind the mic. "I'm not thrilled with how this is coming together. Let's just start from the top."

Jodie nodded, swallowed down a bout of nerves as

she shuffled through the sheet music to find her place. This was the second rehearsal, and it hadn't gone a whole lot better than the one yesterday. Tomorrow was the concert, and Jodie sensed Mandie's frustration with her.

This morning Finn had texted her a fun and encouraging message, and the good mood it had created carried her all the way here, until she saw Amy in her usual spot on the front bench. Every practice, the woman showed up, watching, judging, with waves of silent censure emanating from her.

Jodie wished Aunt Laura would come again. At least then she would feel she had someone on her side. But her aunt had stayed away today and Jodie was on her own.

It's about the music, she told herself, placing her hands on the keys, taking in a deep breath. *Only the music is important.*

She wanted to do a good job. Make Finn proud of her. She wanted to be worthy of him. Her hands faltered and she hit a discordant note and stopped.

Even from here she heard Mandie's suppressed sigh. She knew the singer was being patient, but her frustration was showing.

I'm trying, Jodie wanted to shout. *I'm trying to be the person you want me to be.*

"I think we should take a break," Mandie said with a stilted smile.

"We have coffee and goodies in the hall," Amy said, jumping to her feet. "I'll go get it ready."

"Sounds fantastic," the singer said, unhooking the cordless mic from her ears and setting it carefully on the table beside her music stand. "You coming?" she asked Jodie.

Jodie shook her head. "I want to go over this piece again."

"Good idea." Mandie gave her a tight nod, then left, her entourage trailing behind her, her succinct comment making Jodie feel even worse than she had before.

She sat at the piano, her heart clenching with a mixture of emotions. She missed Finn and she didn't like the feeling. Missing him filled her with doubts and uncertainties. Missing Finn meant he mattered, which meant his opinion of her mattered, which meant she was vulnerable.

It didn't help her flustered state of mind that every time she looked over at Amy she not only felt but saw the disapproval in her eyes.

Jodie shifted the music around, took a breath, closed her eyes and began playing again. She knew most of the pieces by heart; she'd been playing them every night, trying to get them exactly right.

The beautiful songs and lyrics touched her soul. So why couldn't she let those emotions sift into the music?

Because you're not good enough.

Jodie's fingers fumbled and again the jarring notes rang through the emptiness of the church.

"You need to relax."

Aunt Laura's voice startled her and Jodie spun around, so incredibly thankful to see her that she felt like crying.

Her aunt sat down beside her and Jodie gave her a hug, clinging to her.

"Hey, honey, is everything okay?" she asked.

Jodie pulled in a wavering breath, about to tell her

that yes, everything was fine. But she was tired of trying so hard.

"I feel so mixed up and confused." The words tumbled out of her.

"Why is that?" Aunt Laura asked, her voice gentle, encouraging.

Jodie turned back to the piano, her emotions wound up so tightly she couldn't grasp one single thread.

"This used to come so easy," she said with a sigh, carefully picking out the tune. "I would sit at the piano and let the music come out. It would just flow."

Never mind that this often happened in a bar, as opposed to here, where she felt everyone watched, weighed and measured.

But she wasn't about to tell her aunt about that part of her life. Her dear aunt who never had anything stronger to drink than a double espresso.

"I feel like I'm grabbing at the notes, trying to push them into a box," she said, her voice strangled. "They don't fit anymore and I'm trying so hard to make it work."

"That's why it's not working. You can't relax when you're trying that hard," Aunt Laura said. "Music has to flow from within you. Has to be an expression of who you are."

And that's part of the problem, too, Jodie thought. She didn't know who she was anymore. She couldn't go back to who she was before, but didn't know who she should be. Most of her decisions had been a reaction to her circumstances instead of deciding for herself what she wanted.

She felt as if she had been trying to edit herself, hoping people would find this version of her more acceptable than the real thing. And most of all, hoping Finn would find her more acceptable. Because since her conversation with Brooke, lingering behind Finn was the image of Denise. The perfect woman Finn had hoped to marry.

"Could it be you're missing Finn?" Aunt Laura said with a wink. "Should I call him and get him to come back right away?"

Jodie flushed, sensing a deeper question in her aunt's voice. But she wasn't about to bare her soul, only to be told, vaguely or directly, that she wasn't the one for him.

"No. I'll just have to muddle through this on my own." She pulled in a breath, tinkling the keys absently. "I'm sure Mandie is wishing right about now that Finn's mother was playing instead of me."

"Maybe. But that's the other reality. Christie isn't playing because she left her son in the lurch."

"How well do you know Finn's mom? She wasn't around much whenever I was here."

"I know her as well as anyone else in Saddlebank. She has always kept to herself. She left Finn alone far too much. She used to play for church, but would often not show up, which meant I had to cover for her." Laura released a sigh that hinted at Christie Hicks's failings. "I also know much of what Finn does is a reaction to his mother's behavior. A way of showing the people of Saddlebank that his mom may not be dependable, but he is. That though she made bad choices, he doesn't."

While her aunt talked, Jodie played a random melody, comparing her life with Finn's. It seemed neither of them had the best parents. The only difference was that the community was aware of Christie's failings.

"Do you think that's been part of the problem with me and my father?" Jodie asked.

Aunt Laura frowned. "What do you mean?"

She toyed with a few more notes, wondering how to broach the subject. "I sometimes think some of my choices were a reaction to what Dad did…how we got along."

Aunt Laura touched some keys on the high octave of the piano while she seemed to look for the right thing to say. "I doubt any of our choices are purely ours. I think we are always reacting to what other people do to us. You and your father had a complicated relationship."

"That's a diplomatic way to put it," Jodie said. But the words came out harsher than she anticipated.

Her aunt frowned at her. "What do you mean?"

"It doesn't matter." She waved off her question.

"But it does. You know I care about you."

Jodie did know. The last few years she'd summered in Saddlebank, when she came to the ranch without her sisters, her aunt always supported her.

But her thoughts ticked back to the many times she had hesitantly broached the subject of her father's treatment of her. And her aunt's puzzlement. Her veiled disbelief and the very tentative comments that maybe Jodie had brought some of her father's anger on herself with her behavior.

"I know Dad resented us being at the ranch," she murmured. It was all she could say.

"I think he resented the way his life ended up," Aunt Laura stated. "I don't think you know this, but your father had big plans. He wanted to join the marines. Leave Saddlebank. And then he met your mother and they got married, and shortly after that your sisters were born.

Then you. Your mother had a hard time here. And they fought a lot."

"I remember some fights," Jodie said. "Was it all bad?"

"Oh, no. There were good moments."

Jodie drew up her memory of ice cream in the park and smiled.

"Just not enough of them," Aunt Laura continued. "After your mother died and you girls started coming here in the summers, I think he felt lost. He told me from time to time that he wasn't always sure what to do with you. Especially once you hit your teens."

"Especially once I hit my teens," Jodie added. "We butted heads a lot."

"So you said."

Once again Jodie felt a quiet dismissal of what she had endured, living with her father. The disbelief that she had written about in a song she'd been fooling with.

The song was a way of saying what no one would hear. A catharsis.

Aunt Laura picked up Jodie's hand, turning it so she could see the scar on the back. "He never said anything about how you got hurt, but I know it ate away at him that you missed your audition because of it. He knew what it meant to you."

Her comment only added to Jodie's confusion.

"I had always hoped you would try again," Aunt Laura said.

"What do you mean?"

"Apply again. Audition again."

"That was my only chance," Jodie said, unable to keep the defensive tone out of her voice.

"Was it?"

Aunt Laura let the question settle between them and Jodie didn't like the other questions it raised.

"Why don't you try this piece again," her aunt prompted after a few seconds of silence, changing the subject. "I've heard you play many times. You have a gift that I feel you're stifling. Don't try to play the songs, try to play the music. Let the words soak in and inspire you, and let them come out in the music. Close your eyes. Close off your memories. Just be here and now. My dearest Jodie, playing a beautiful piece of music the way you know how. Stop trying to be who you think you should be. Just be Jodie."

"Trouble is, I don't know who Jodie is anymore," she said, sorrow plucking at her with every note she fingered on the keyboard. "Lately I feel as if I'm trying to be someone I'm not."

"Is that why you're wearing this somber getup?" Aunt Laura asked. "Instead of the fun and exciting clothes you always wear?"

"Maybe."

"Well, this isn't you, either. And I think you need to know how important it is to accept who you truly are and bring that to the music. Don't try to edit or stifle yourself, trying to put forth a version that you think everyone will like. Don't play for me. Or Finn. Or Amy. I want you to know that the gift you've been given comes from God. He's the one you should be playing for. No one else."

"But it's Mandie's music," Jodie protested.

"Yes. But she wrote it for God. To praise Him. And that's who you should play for."

"Trouble is, I don't feel as though I'm worthy of Him, either."

"None of us are," Laura said. "That's what grace is all about. As C. S. Lewis says, 'We don't believe God will love us because we are good, but that God will make us good because He loves us.' And that's what this song is about. God helping us as we stumble into grace. Making us weak humans good."

Jodie placed her hands on the keyboard and found the tune, hesitantly at first, as if blindly feeling her way through a new piece. As if discovering this song anew. The notes took shape and form in her mind, and as she found the music, found the soul of it, she felt the same emotions she had the first time. The heartache, the hungering.

Jodie imagined her weary footsteps moving toward a God who wanted to make her good. And as she imagined His arms held out to her, the music pulled her toward Him, drawing them together.

She felt her aunt's arm around her shoulders and once again felt her unconditional love.

"It's not about you," Aunt Laura said as Jodie played, letting the music pull her along. "It's about God and about using your gifts to serve Him. To give back to Him what He gave to you. Forget about the people and their expectations. Think of yourself as giving yourself to God. Just Jodie. As you are right now."

Jodie breathed in, taking charge of the music and bringing herself into it. Bringing her experiences, her emotions, her needs and wants. And as she played she felt as if the music was finally freed.

"Just like that," her aunt said. "Exactly like that."

Jodie smiled, and it seemed not only was her aunt's arm around her shoulder, it was as if God held her closely, as well.

She wanted to accept it. To let God's love make her new.

She thought of Finn and all that might be if she made a choice to do better. To be better.

But did she dare put herself in that vulnerable position again?

Chapter Fourteen

"I missed you," Finn said. "I'm just pulling in to the ranch now. I'll be at the church as soon as possible."

"I missed you, too," Jodie said, pressing her phone to her ear as she sat down on the bed in her old room, unable to stop smiling at the sound of his voice. It frightened her how much she had missed him after spending such a short time with him.

Frightened and thrilled her.

"So I heard that Mandie was happy with how your practice went yesterday. Inspired, in fact."

His comment underlined the enthusiasm she had heard from Mandie both in the second half of the rehearsal on Thursday and the dress rehearsal this morning. Somehow, Jodie had figured out how to blank Amy out and keep her mind on her music.

"I got some help from Aunt Laura."

"What did she do?"

"Encouraged me to be myself."

"Best person to be," Finn said.

"Something else interesting happened last night."

"Tell me," he urged.

"When I thought everyone was gone, I was just fooling around, playing one of my compositions, and Mandie came back to get something she forgot. She heard me play and said she wanted to hear more." Jodie stopped there, still not sure what to make of the singer's encouragement. In fact, Mandie wanted to add one of her songs to the concert.

"That's amazing. I'm so happy that someone else had a chance to see your talent." Finn's excitement seemed to solidify the fragile dreams Jodie had harbored the nights she dared play her own music in the bars, knowing that most of the people wouldn't judge and didn't care. Dreams that somehow, somewhere, she could do more with this.

Could this be her opportunity?

"I'm so sorry I couldn't be there for that myself," Finn continued, his enthusiasm making her feel whole. "I'm so glad I'll be seeing you in an hour or so. I've got some good news to share, too."

And why did her heart start pounding against her chest at that?

"Sounds mysterious. Any hints?"

"It's about our…my future."

She didn't think she imagined that slip of his tongue, but didn't dare press him on it.

A future? With her?

The thought made her heart beat faster with the same mixture of anticipation and fear she had just felt.

"But I gotta go," Finn continued. "I promised Brooke I'd help her get everything set up. I'll see you soon." His pause made her think he wanted to say something else. But he only said goodbye, then ended the call.

Jodie stayed on her bed, still holding the phone as if

reluctant to break the connection with Finn. The chiming of a clock reminded her that she had to get going. She put on a pair of simple silver hoop earrings, redid her lipstick and gave herself a quick once-over in the mirror.

She had decided on a simple black dress that she had found in the thrift store in Saddlebank. She had cut off the sleeves, turning it into a basic shift. An elaborately embroidered scarf draped around her shoulders and held in place with a pin in the shape of a musical note was her individual stamp on the outfit.

She skimmed her hand over her dress, feeling a touch of disloyalty to her old self. She wanted to show Finn that she knew how to adjust. How to blend in.

Couldn't you just expect him to love the real you?

She felt a sudden jolt of fear. *The real me.* Who was that?

She shook her head and headed down the stairs. In the living room she gathered her music from the piano and tried to fit it into the envelope. But the worn envelope ripped, so she went into her father's office to find a new one.

Jodie opened drawers and cupboards, but couldn't find any. She glanced at the filing cabinet. She hadn't looked in there yet, unable to get past the idea that by doing so she would invade her father's last stronghold of privacy.

But she needed an envelope, and she found a stack in the lower drawer. She took one off the top.

Then was puzzled when she turned it over to put the sheet music inside. It had her name scribbled on it, but was empty. Puzzled, she turned to the other envelopes. Another one had her name on it, and her grandmother's address, but again, nothing inside. She went through the stack. Some had Erin's name, some Lauren's, all empty. Then, at the bottom of the pile, she found a fat, worn envelope. This one was full of papers.

Jodie pulled it out of the cabinet and took it to the kitchen, laying it on the island there.

Just as she did, she caught sight of the clock. Time to go.

She returned to the office, snatched an empty envelope and shoved her music inside. She'd look at the papers later.

Finn pulled into the church parking lot, glancing at the clock on the dashboard.

Half an hour until the concert started. He had enough time to give Jodie a little pep talk, help Brooke do some setup in the hall, and then he could relax and, hopefully, enjoy the concert.

He had spoken with his mother, encouraged her once again to come up to Saddlebank for the concert.

He had been going nonstop since he'd trailered the horse he had been training up to Great Falls. Finn had spent some time there with his client, going over some of the training he had done, making sure she was comfortable with the horse. Then, as soon as was polite, he'd hurried back to the ranch to drop off the trailer and clean up. But before he did that, he'd stopped at Dr. Wilkinson's and finalized the deal they had talked about over the phone on his way up to Great Falls.

He still couldn't believe he had done it. He was going to be the owner of a piece of property. His own ranch.

His head still spun, second thoughts chasing third thoughts.

You were going to do it eventually, he reminded himself.

You ditched your ten-year plan, another voice told him.

But somehow, this felt right. As if his life was falling into a good place.

He had almost told Jodie when he called her, but he wanted to say it in person. And now he was here with enough time to tell her, give her a pep talk and then relax and enjoy the concert.

He gave himself a once-over in the mirror, noticed a spot that he'd missed shaving, then laughed at himself. Jodie would have to take him as he was.

As he got out of the truck, he heard the muted notes of a piano. Jodie going over the music. His heart quickened,

As Finn walked toward the church, he saw his mother waiting for him just outside the door. Her hair was pulled back in a low bun. She wore a gray, flowing dress and pink cardigan.

"Hey, Mom. You came. Are you coming in?" he asked, holding his arm out to accompany her.

She bit her lip, looking from him to the entrance of the church, then shrugged. "Maybe. In a bit."

He stifled a beat of annoyance at her hesitancy. He was so sure she would come.

"I just need a few moments," she said, twisting her hands around each other.

Finn wanted to give them to her, but he was anxious to see Jodie. He fought down the urgency that grabbed at him. The obligations waiting.

He sensed his mom had something she wanted to tell him. Experience had taught him to give her time to formulate either her excuses or another apology, or any other reason she couldn't do whatever she had promised she would do.

"Do you need to tell me something?" he prompted.

She nodded. "Yes. Yes I do." A bit more hand fiddling and then she shot him an apologetic look. "You need to know that I've been trying to change things in my life. I wanted to tell you the last time I was here. I didn't dare."

Finn kept quiet, thinking of the fact that Jodie was now playing a concert his mother was supposed to, but had suddenly quit.

She took a breath and looked up at him. "I've been seeing a counselor."

Finn just stared at her. This was not what he expected.

"Really. Why?" Though as soon as he spoke the question he knew he could safely assume it had something to do with her unreliability. "Does this have to do with Dad's death?"

It wasn't until Denise died that he understood, to a small degree, what his mother must have gone through. The loss, the grieving. But he had been grieving, too. And he knew that his disappointments with her were older than that. Her absences were common. They just got worse after his father died.

"Partly." She swallowed, her slender fingers, still wearing her wedding ring, worrying at the hem of her sweater. She pulled in another breath. "When I canceled on this concert, I knew I had to do something about my…my problem. I knew I couldn't handle it on my own anymore. So I started seeing a counselor." She looked up at him now, her expression holding a plea for understanding. "I've been struggling with depression all my life. I managed to keep it from you. Your father had an idea, but he was of the 'ignore it and it will go away' camp. We never had...had the best relationship, but he was a good man. I just wasn't the wife he had hoped I would be. I wanted to go to your school plays and baseball games and all the rest. And each time, I promised myself I would, yet when the time actually came...I couldn't. I just couldn't." She looked as if she was about to apologize again, but stopped herself. "It was the depression. That's why I never got as far with my music as I should have. I would freeze up when opportunities came along. I never knew when it would happen. I thought I would be able to do this concert, but I was afraid that I would be able to do the rehearsals and then fail you when the time came for the actual performance."

"You've been struggling with depression?" Finn tried to absorb this. "Why didn't you tell me sooner?" As soon as he spoke the words, he regretted them.

Too much going on, he told himself. Jodie. The concert. Buying the ranch. It made his head tired.

"It would have made such a difference if I had known," he continued. "Why did you keep this a secret from me?"

"I was ashamed to tell you." She gave him a wavering smile that he knew far too well.

Please forgive me, it begged.

He dragged his hand over his face and exhaled, as if trying to find his center in this place his mother had brought him with her confession.

Depression. It explained so much.

A flash of anger gripped him at his mother's… deception? Could he call it that?

If he had known, would he have been so condemning of her?

Guilt mingled with frustration flowed through him.

"You should have told me sooner," he said quietly.

A few more vehicles pulled into the parking lot. People were starting to arrive. The music from the auditorium had quit. He had to get going. Brooke was waiting.

And more important, Jodie.

"Let's go inside," he said. "We can talk more later."

His mother's expression told him that, once again, she was going to disappoint him. "I have to leave after the performance."

Of course she did.

"Well, come into the hall and enjoy the concert. Jodie is an amazing pianist," he said.

Christie took his arm, nodding. "I'm glad she got the opportunity. I always thought she had a lot of promise."

Finn nodded as they walked into the church together.

And he was surprised how nice it felt.

Finn sat back, awash in satisfaction as Mandie's voice reverberated through the auditorium. Weaving in and around it were the notes of the piano, enhancing, building.

Jodie sat at the keyboard, looking transfixed as her fingers unerringly found the song, putting herself into the music. She had worn her hair loose tonight, flowing over the shoulders of her simple black dress, the pin holding her flamboyant scarf flashing in the overhead lights. The plain dress surprised him, but the scarf and pin were pure Jodie.

Mandie's backup singers and the guitar and drums accompanying her were a mere footnote to what happened between Jodie and Mandie. They played off each other, the piano notes and the singer's voice entwined, as if one.

Then, her expression rapt, Mandie raised her hands as she delivered the last bars of the final number, singing her song of praise to God. Jodie played a final crescendo, then faded away, leaving Mandie's clear voice to hold the last of the melody.

Utter silence followed, and then people surged to their feet, applauding wildly.

Finn joined them, his mother beside him, clapping as loudly as everyone else. Finn couldn't stop smiling as Mandie took a bow. Then another. And then reached out for Jodie to come and join her. Jodie got up from the piano and walked to her side, and holding hands, they bowed.

Finn was so proud. Jodie's smile was broad, open, natural. And then her eyes wandered over the gathering, as if looking for him. If anything, her smile widened.

Finn wanted to hold on to this moment. The connection between him and Jodie, the satisfaction of the success of the concert. The joy of the music.

It all came together in the same perfect harmony that he had just witnessed between Jodie and Mandie.

In that moment he was thankful his mother hadn't played. He shot her a glance, surprised to see the genuine joy on her face. Then felt a surprising peace and contentment.

Though he was frustrated with his mother's delay in telling him about her struggles, he was glad she finally had been honest with him. It explained so much.

Slowly the applause died down, and Mandie once again thanked everyone for coming, reminding them of the refreshments waiting in the hall.

Finn turned to his mother. "Are you coming with me? I want to say hi to Jodie."

But he saw from the way Christie fiddled with her fingers that it wasn't happening.

Though she had explained why, he still couldn't understand what she dealt with.

"I should go," she said. "I'll call you."

"Where are you going?"

"Back to Bozeman."

"Will you be returning soon? I don't want you to drop out of my life again. I just bought Doc Wilkinson's place, and I want you to come visit me."

"I'll see," she said simply.

He held her hands and looked into her eyes. "I'm not making you promise me, but I really want you to come."

She met his gaze and he saw hope there. "I'll try. I'll call you."

Then she walked away from him, again, not looking back.

Finn watched her go, then turned to where Jodie stood at the front of the church, accepting people's congratulations. He hung back, not wanting to take this moment from her.

Finally he couldn't wait any longer and hurried through the people to her side, anxious to be with her. To hold her.

"That was awesome," he said, taking her hands in his. They were warm, soft, and she clung to his in turn, her eyes locked on his. "You were inspiring. Gave me shivers to listen to you play."

"Thanks so much," she said. Her eyes shone a silvery blue in the subdued lighting on the stage and she gave him a tremulous smile. "I missed you."

He tucked his knuckle under her chin, lifting her face to his. "You've been an inspiration to me," he said. "Especially the way you played tonight. Tonight I saw the Jodie that I know and care for more than I thought possible."

Her smile dived into his heart and settled there.

She caught his arm and, in spite of the people still milling about, kissed him, and Finn felt as if everything in his life had come together, perfectly tied up in this moment.

He held her close, tucking her head into his shoulder, not caring who saw.

"*Did* you miss me?" he asked, stroking her hair.

"A lot," she said. "I'm so glad you're here."

"This woman is amazing," Mandie said, coming to join them. "I'm not going to lie, I had my reservations at first, but she came through."

Finn felt awash in pride. "I'm glad."

The singer turned to Jodie. "I'll be in town a couple of days yet. We need to talk about your music."

Jodie nodded, her smile so wide Finn thought her face would crack in half. "That would be wonderful."

Mandie gave her a pat on the shoulder and sent Finn a broad smile. "Thanks for asking her to play. She's got an unbelievable gift."

Finn wanted nothing more than to take Jodie away, pull her from this crowd and give her his good news.

But people kept coming forward, congratulating her, and he knew he couldn't interrupt this public affirmation of what she had just done. Maybe the support she felt would pull her further into the community he hoped she would allow herself to be a part of.

Fifteen minutes later the crowd thinned and Jodie and Finn had another moment to themselves.

"There's coffee, tea and punch in the hall. I'm sure you're parched," he said as they slowly walked through the quickly emptying auditorium. Chatter from the foyer and the hall beyond drifted toward them.

"A bit," she admitted. But her steps slowed as they walked down the carpeted aisle. She didn't seem in any rush to join the postconcert celebration. Then she turned to him. "How was your trip? I'm sorry, I didn't even have a chance to ask."

"It was good. Carrie, my customer, was thrilled with the horse. Gave me some more business. I might have to tap into your dad's herd," he said.

"I might have to charge you for that," she returned, a twinkle in her eyes. "Those are good horses. Some very well-trained horses," she added, tucking her arm in his.

He held her gaze, sensing they hovered on the verge of something. A new step. He knew where he stood. He wanted to make sure, before he made any kind of declaration, that Jodie occupied the same space.

"I have some good news to tell you later that will make you proud of me," he said. "About my place."

"Sounds mysterious," she answered, giving him a coy look.

The sanctuary was nearly empty now, but Finn wasn't ready to leave. He waited until the last stragglers left, then turned to Jodie to satisfy a curiosity that one of the songs had created.

"I found that second-to-last song you and Mandie played interesting. I never heard it before."

He hadn't heard it any of the times he'd stopped by the rehearsals. There was something haunting about it. A bit disturbing, even. He wanted to know more about it.

Jodie smiled. "That's because I wrote it."

"Really?" He tilted his head to one side, as if seeing her from a new angle. "That's amazing."

"It was a last-minute addition. Mandie really wanted to sing it. She heard me playing it one afternoon and wanted to add it to the set list."

Finn looked at Jodie and sensed a vulnerability.

"The chorus was interesting," he said. "'Old wounds and old scars, stories pushed aside. Disbelief and unbelief, keeping secrets inside.' That sounded kind of vague, and yet I have a feeling you were trying to say something."

Jodie waved him off. "It was just a song about someone dealing with the past."

"Your past?" he pressed.

"Oh…no…"

"What was that song about?"

"It was a just a song. About…loss." But as she spoke she ran her fingers over the back of her hand, tracing her scar.

"Your loss? Your wounds?"

She simply shrugged, but he noticed she didn't deny that it might be true.

"What did you mean by disbelief and unbelief? Keeping secrets?" He felt it was some subliminal message that was easier to deliver in the music.

Then she looked at him, an expression of sorrow and resignation crossing her face.

"You don't want to know about my dad. Not yet."

Her dad? What did she mean by that? Finn had said nothing about her father.

He held her gaze as the movements of her fingers grew more agitated, and he felt as if cogs were slowly clicking into place.

Finn thought of all the evasive comments Jodie had made about her father. He knew they were on the verge of something important. His mind ticked back to his mother and the secret she had thrown at him, and he was suddenly tired of being left out of the loop like some child that needed to be protected.

"Please tell me, Jodie," he said, an edge of anger creeping into his voice. "I insist."

He didn't want their relationship to go any further until they could clear things up.

"You insist?"

He knew that was the wrong word as soon as he spoke it, but he stood his ground. "I'd like to know."

Jodie held his gaze, her eyes growing flat. And for a moment he wondered if he had pushed too hard.

"I don't want any more secrets," he pressed, suddenly weary. "I've had enough of them. I need to know the truth."

That came out harsher than he wanted it to, but he was still dealing with what his mother had told him and how it changed his perception of her.

Now it seemed Jodie had secrets, as well.

"Tell me," he said.

In answer, she held up her hand, the one with the scar on the back. The scar she never talked about. Once again he remembered her walking around with a bandage on her hand. Walking around with Jaden Woytuk.

"I never told you how I got this." She paused for an

instant, looking down at it. "It happened the night before I was supposed to go for my audition. The night we were supposed to meet each other. I liked you, but I was scared because you were a decent guy, and I couldn't imagine why you wanted to be with me. We'd already had a couple of dates. But my dad found out. He told me that you were too good for me, and the trouble was, I believed him. So instead of going out on our date, I went to Jaden's for a party. Jaden always understood me," she said.

"But once I was at the party, I realized that my father was wrong. I maybe didn't deserve you, but I had a right to be happy, too. And I realized how silly I felt attending this stupid party. But just as I was leaving to go and find you, my father came in to bust the party. He saw me, started yelling, as he usually did, and I yelled back like I usually did." She stopped, her voice breaking as she looked down at the scar on her hand. "That's when it happened. He shoved me. I fell and cut my hand on a broken bottle. Instead of arresting me, he brought me to the hospital. I didn't make our date, and I couldn't go to my audition with an injured hand. It was my father's fault I missed that audition. It was because of him that I cut my hand."

"I don't understand why... I can't imagine that he would—"

"He did it because my dad had a hard time with me." Jodie interrupted his stunned comments, her voice emotionless. "He never thought I was good enough. What happened that night was more of the same in our relationship. He used to hit me when he got angry with me. Sometimes with an open hand. A couple of times with his belt, when he was punishing me. That was what my life with my father was like. I didn't miss the audition because I didn't care. I missed it because my father was angry with me and pushed me. And I cut my hand. I missed our date because he didn't think I was good enough for you."

Finn shook his head as he tried to envision the man who had done so much for him acting as Jodie was describing. His mind was awash with confusion as he said, "I don't think I can believe this."

Chapter Fifteen

Jodie just stared at Finn. His words were like weapons, stabbing at her. The doubt in his voice, his incredulous expression reminiscent of the disbelief she'd seen on Lane's face, her father's steady accusations of lying— she couldn't separate it all.

I don't think I can believe this.

"You think I'm not g-good enough to believe?" That was all she could stammer out.

Finn frowned at her. "What?"

"I know I'm not like your precious Denise. I never will be."

"I don't expect that, but your dad, he was… I can't imagine…" Finn stopped there and ice seemed to flow through Jodie's veins.

"You're choosing my father over me." She shook her head, then took a step back. Why was she surprised?

"I have to go," she said. "Don't bother following me. I don't need this."

"Jodie. Are you really leaving?"

She couldn't stay and look at the skepticism in his eyes, hear the doubt in his voice.

Be the first to leave. That way you don't get hurt.

"I'm serious. Just leave me alone. It's over," she said. Then she turned and ran down the aisle toward the back exit of the church building.

She wasn't sure how she made it to her car across the dark parking lot. The only thing she knew was that when she saw the look of disbelief on Finn's face, when she heard him put a voice to it, she had to go.

She twisted the key in the ignition, then slammed the car into gear, her lights bouncing off a few concert-goers who'd opted out of the postperformance coffee.

She was halfway to the ranch when her phone buzzed from her purse. She slowed down and pulled it out, glanced at her call display. Aunt Laura.

Jodie chided herself. Did she seriously expect Finn to call her after she'd dropped that on him and then walked away?

She had to. Once she had seen his expression of disbelief, she simply couldn't put herself through that again.

By the time she got to the house she felt as if she had run a marathon. Exhaustion clawed at her and she wanted nothing more than to drop onto her bed, close her eyes and sink away into mindless sleep.

She pulled open the door, and as she did it was as if all the negative echoes of her father's condemnation she had spent the past few weeks eradicating thundered back at her, and she had to face them alone.

No good. Useless. Troublemaker.

And the worst one.

Liar.

She tossed her purse on the kitchen island, then trudged into her room, fighting the tears that threatened. Too many men had made her cry in her lifetime. She couldn't let one more have that power over her.

But Finn wasn't just any man. She knew, deep in her soul, that he was a man she had dared to pin hopes on.

She didn't like feeling this way. It hurt even more than after she and Lane had broken up. It cut deep into a part of her that she thought she had closed off.

Foolish girl.

She picked up her phone. Looking at it, she thought of all the men who'd had control over her life and her emotions. She fought down her sorrow. Not again. She wasn't going to be the one left behind again. The one told she wasn't good enough. This time she was in charge.

Fighting the urge to call her sister, she pulled up Finn's number.

Call him.

She couldn't do it.

So she sent him a text.

Leaving tomorrow. Need a break.

Before she could change her mind she hit Send, then set her phone aside.

She would call Drake Neubauer tomorrow and find out what would happen to her share of the ranch if she didn't stay the entire two months.

"Wonderful concert," Heather Argall said to Finn as she took the glass of punch he offered her.

"Thanks. I thought it went well." He gave Heather an inane smile, looking beyond her to the people still milling about.

The hall adjoining the church was packed, noisy and

filled with a jubilance that he should have been celebrating.

Instead, for the past hour all he thought of was Jodie's unexpected bomb and how she'd run off before he could talk to her about it.

Running away instead of staying around to deal with it. Just like his mom.

Drop this secret into his life, expect him to cope and then leave.

He knew his anger with Jodie was mixed in with the older resentment he felt toward his mother, as well as the confusion that Jodie's comments had created.

Doubt niggled at him, followed by a feeling of disloyalty. He had appreciated Keith McCauley in his life. Had always prided himself on being loyal to the man who had helped him so much. But Jodie had thrown that all into turmoil.

And she had kept it a secret from him. Didn't she trust him?

"I can tell you, Jodie was a surprise," Heather said, snagging his attention. "I knew she played the piano, but I never knew she was so talented. Too bad Keith couldn't have heard her."

Yes. What would Keith have thought?

"Well, I better get moving, let you serve a few more people. Great turnout, too." Heather gave him another smile and then Finn was serving the next person, who was as fulsome in his appreciation of the concert.

In the far corner of the hall Mandie Parker held court, laughing and smiling, looking very pleased.

This should have made Finn feel better, but all he could think of was the look on Jodie's face after she'd dropped her bomb. How she'd become angry, then run off, leaving him behind to absorb what she'd said.

Keith? The man he admired so much had abused his own daughter?

Finn still couldn't put the two together, and yet the way Jodie talked, he knew she wasn't just making this up. He needed some space to think this all through. A picture of Keith hitting Jodie jumped into his mind. He couldn't process it. He needed to talk to her.

But first he had to take care of his obligations here. Be the responsible citizen Keith had always encouraged him to be.

It seemed hours before Finn refilled the last punch cup, made the last bit of small talk, but in truth it was only sixty minutes. People started leaving and he still had to clean up.

"Finn? Are you okay?"

Mandie's voice broke through his thoughts. He sent up a ragged prayer for help and patience, then turned to face the woman who a short time ago had held an entire auditorium in thrall with her voice.

"You did a fantastic job," he said with heartfelt enthusiasm. "Thanks so much for a mesmerizing performance."

"Couldn't have done it without Jodie. Have you seen her? I need to talk to her."

"I just got a text from her. She won't be coming back tonight." Amazing how casual he sounded when his heart beat heavier than the bass drum of Mandie's backup group.

"Why not? Everyone wants to congratulate her. She did such an outstanding job. You must be so proud of her."

"I am."

"Do you have her phone number?" Mandie gave him

a grateful smile. "I'm so glad that we persevered with her. Something happened the past few days that made her relax and let us see the real talent she'd been hiding. She played a couple of her compositions for me last night after our rehearsal. Astounding talent. Don't know if you noticed, but we performed one tonight."

Oh, he had noticed, all right.

Finn recited Jodie's number as Mandie typed it into her phone. Then she looked up, frowning at him. "You look upset. Is everything okay?"

Nothing was okay. Everything was wrong.

"I'll be fine. Just coming down off a lot of stress with this festival." He forced a wan smile. "It went well, but I'm looking forward to some quiet time."

"You deserve it." Mandie patted him on his shoulder and gave him an encouraging smile. "Is your mother still here? I was so sure I saw her with you."

"No. She's gone, too." Finn's smile became even more forced. Coming on the heels of Jodie's current defection, he didn't want the reminder of how capricious the women in his life were.

Mandie tightened her hand on his shoulder. "Sorry to hear that. She called me a while back to apologize for leaving me in the lurch. But truth to tell, I'm glad she did. Jodie was amazing."

Finn just nodded, feeling more weary than he had in years.

The evening was not supposed to begin and end the way it had, bracketed by confessions from his mother and Jodie.

He needed time and space to process all these revelations.

He needed to get home.

Chapter Sixteen

The darkness that filled the house was eased by the reading light above the chair Jodie had retreated to after she sent her text to Finn. She had changed into a caftan she'd bought in Israel and a pair of leggings she had picked up from a thrift store. She had packed her suitcase.

Now what? Was she really leaving tomorrow?

Jodie closed her eyes, massaging her temples. When she'd seen the disbelief in his eyes, when she'd heard him express it, she'd known she couldn't stick around.

It had been hard enough to deal with that from Lane.

Seeing it on Finn's face had cut like a knife.

She wasn't sure she could stay. She would have to wait until morning to talk to her father's lawyer and find out what the implications would be if she left before her time was up.

You need to give Finn a chance.

For what? To tell her yet again how wonderful her father was? Make her feel she wasn't worthy of being believed?

The questions dogged her and she got up to make

herself some hot chocolate. She filled the kettle with water, put it on the stove to boil and scooped some powder into a large mug she had gotten from Aunt Laura for one of her birthdays. It had a picture of a swaybacked horse staring back at her, and below it the caption, I'm Built for Comfort, Not Speed.

Aunt Laura.

Should she call her?

The clock showed her it was too late to do that. Maybe tomorrow morning.

Jodie stirred the boiling water into the cocoa, watching it melt. She wouldn't sleep tonight anyway. Each time she closed her eyes, she imagined Finn's face as she'd told him about her father. Lifting her mug, she blew on the hot chocolate, and through the steam looked over at her father's office.

Her dad had done so much to her. Broken so much in her life. She could hear, like an echo, his accusations. *Little liar. Little sneak. Useless little girl.*

She felt the fear and anger build up as she wondered how it would end.

Jodie had told herself she wasn't going to cry, but the unwelcome tears coursed down her face.

Her eyes fell on the envelope she had set on the counter this afternoon.

Before everything had fallen apart.

She needed a distraction, so she grabbed it, took it to the dining room and sat down at the table. She set her mug aside and opened the large envelope. As she pulled the stack of papers out, a bundle of canceled checks came with them.

The top one was dated the year she, her mother and her sisters left the farm. And it was made out to her mom. Puzzled, Jodie riffled through the rest of the checks. Every month, on the first, her father had sent money. When her mother died, the checks were made out to their grandmother.

Jodie felt her world shift when she saw them. Neither her mother nor her grandmother had ever said anything or even hinted at the fact that their father had sent them money.

She set the checks aside and picked up the papers he had been working on. Once more she felt a tiny jolt when she saw her father's handwriting. Neat, tidy and upright. Just like the man he presented to the world. The man Finn believed he was.

The first letter was addressed to Lauren. The second to Erin. These Jodie slipped into envelopes for her sisters, resisting the temptation to read them. They weren't for her eyes.

The remaining five were addressed to her.

"Dear Jodie," the first one began. Then a bunch of lines were crossed out. A few lines stating how hard it was to see her behave the way she did were also scratched through.

The next letter was almost identical, as was the third. Puzzled, she read through the marked-up lines. More about her behavior and how hard it was to see her challenge him all the time. She almost didn't read the fifth one, but when she took it out she didn't see any writing scratched out.

"Dear Jodie," she read.

I'm not good at this kind of thing. Never was. But I'm dying and that has made me think about things. Eternity is staring me in the face and it's making me look back at what I did. I wasn't a good father to you. I was an angry man. Your mother used to cheat on me and for a while I thought you weren't mine.

Jodie's heart did a double flip at her father's blunt words.

She tried to make sense of them, then shook her head as if to rearrange her thoughts and read on.

"I found out that wasn't true. I confess. I did a DNA test to find out."

DNA test?

She set the letter aside, rubbing her temples. It was too much for one night. Too much to absorb.

She got up and walked around the house. It was as if her entire world had been tossed around like a box of blocks and she couldn't put it back the way it was.

She wanted to call her sister, but hesitated. Who knew what was in Lauren's letter?

Please, Lord...

The feeble plea fell from her lips, and as she made another round she saw the corner of her father's Bible poking out of a pile of books.

Like a desert wanderer thirsting for nourishment, Jodie pulled it from the stack and dropped onto the floor.

Her father always read the Bible when they were here. It wasn't unfamiliar.

She turned to Psalms, remembering their rhythms and cadences. The cries for help that often mirrored her own. Which was the one the pastor read on Sunday?

She turned to Psalm 32.

Blessed is the one whose transgressions are forgiven,

whose sins are covered. Blessed is the one whose sin the Lord does not count against them and in whose spirit is no deceit.

Blessed. Forgiven.

She and her father had had an adversarial relationship. He had always accused and never believed. She had started breaking the rules because her father hadn't believed her when she'd said she hadn't done anything, and would punish her anyway.

But reading this reminded her that she had been looking to the wrong relationship for affirmation.

She thought back to what the pastor had said about how God offered forgiveness. About the unconditional love God offered in Christ, and a chance to start new.

Was this chance now?

And Finn? Where did he fit?

She thought again of the look on his face.

Did it matter that he believed her?

She covered her own face with her hands. "It shouldn't, but it does so much. I just need someone to be on my side," she whispered.

She turned back to the passage. *You are my hiding place.*

"Forgive me, Lord," she prayed. "Forgive me for moving away from You. I confess I haven't lived the kind of life I should and I have been angry with my father, but…" She stopped there, trying not to find an excuse for what she had done. She had made her own choices. "All I can say is I was wrong. Forgive me and help me to trust in You. To know that You are my hiding place. Help me to trust You and to know You are all I need."

She stopped again, and a gentle peace suffused her.

Her life hadn't changed, but she knew Jesus was with her, offering her hope and forgiveness. Taking her as she was.

She stayed a moment, then got up, still holding the Bible, and brought it back to the table and her father's unfinished letter. She had to see this to the end.

She picked the letter up again, the paper crackling in the silence, and read on.

Apologizing about what happened to your hand won't change anything. If I had believed you when you said you were leaving the party, maybe things would have been different. I was an angry man and we always fought. I let my temper get the best of me too many times. Every time I hit you, I felt horrible, but didn't know how to fix it. I guess I'm trying now. I know God has forgiven me for what I did, but that's not enough. I want you to forgive me, too.

His signature was scrawled across the bottom and then, under that, two words. "I'm sorry."

Jodie sat back, her heart thundering in her chest.

Her father? The never wrong Keith McCauley, asking for her forgiveness? Telling her he was sorry? Words she'd never in her whole life thought he would say, let alone write down?

If it weren't for the fact that she recognized her father's handwriting, she would have doubted this even came from him.

She read it again, as if to make sure, but the words hadn't changed. Confusion did battle with vindication as she set the letter down beside the canceled checks he had sent to her mother and grandmother.

Had Jodie looked at her life through the wrong end of binoculars all these years? Making things distant and distorted? *What do I do with this?* she wondered.

Stumbling toward grace...

The words returned to her and she tried to apply them to her father's life, catching a momentary glimpse of the man Finn had seen.

Why couldn't she have seen that side of him? Why had Finn been given that privilege and not her?

Thoughts of Finn mingled with the new revelations from her father.

Finn.

A sharp ache pressed against her chest, making her stomach roil and her head spin.

Tears threatened, but she fought them down. She had promised herself she would never shed tears over another man. But Finn wasn't just another man.

He was the man she had dared weave impossible dreams around.

Her lips trembled and her hands clenched and then her chest heaved.

And the tears she had fought valiantly to keep at bay flowed.

Leaving tomorrow. Need a break.

Finn tossed his cell phone aside and dropped onto the couch, looking around his living room, a feeling of emptiness gripping him.

Since Jodie had sent him that terse text, he didn't know what to think.

She couldn't even stick around to find out how he felt about what she had told him.

He laid his head back and closed his eyes, wishing he knew what to do.

Part of him wanted to go running over to the Rocking M Ranch. To plead with Jodie to stay. But he had done that so often with his mother, he wasn't sure he had the energy to do it again. If Jodie didn't want to stay, he couldn't make her.

Could he?

And what about what she'd told him? About Keith? What should he do with that?

He tried to fit his memories with what Jodie had said. Yes, Keith had a temper, but to hit his own daughter? Keith had helped Finn so much. How could he be the same person Jodie had described?

But if Finn didn't believe her, where did that leave them?

He walked to the darkened window, his ghostly reflection layered over the yard, which was lit up by the light at the peak of the barn.

What do I do with this, Lord? he prayed. *Keith has done so much for me. Is it disloyal to believe what Jodie told me?*

Finn let that thought settle a moment. Then his phone rang and his heart jumped. Jodie?

It was Vic.

"Hey, buddy," Finn said when he answered. "What can I do for you?"

"Sorry for calling so late, but I'm not sure what's happening. I just got a strange phone call from Jodie."

Finn stood up straight, clutching the phone. "What did she want?"

"She was wondering if I could come and feed the horses tomorrow. Is she going somewhere?"

Ice bloomed in Finn's chest. *Leaving tomorrow. Need a break.*

He needed to talk to her about what she'd told him. And she just wanted to leave?

How pathetic was he, thinking that Jodie would have a change of heart? She had told him many times that she didn't like to stick around. That she needed to keep moving.

He had foolishly believed that he could make her change.

"What gives? I thought you were training them," Vic continued. "Getting them ready for her to sell privately."

"When did she call you?"

"Just a few minutes ago."

Finn looked at the clock. It was nearing midnight. "I can't believe she phoned you this late."

"I was up anyway. Dean's not feeling good. Been struggling with a lot of pain lately."

In spite of his own troubles Finn sensed the tension in his friend. Vic felt responsible for Dean's rodeo accident, even though Finn had tried again and again to convince him otherwise. He also knew that Vic, who had been leasing Keith's place, hoped to purchase it eventually, and now that was all up in the air.

"So do you think she still wants to sell the ranch?" Vic asked. "'Cause Keith and I had an agreement and I'm not sure how hard to push that."

"Did you get it in writing?"

His friend sighed. "No. I thought he might have told the girls. That guy was hard to pin down."

And hard to figure out, Finn thought.

He fought down his confusion, not sure what he could or should say. But he needed to talk to someone, if only to get their reaction, as well.

"Jodie told me something that I don't know what to do with," Finn said.

"You sound worried."

He looked over at the mantel, at the pictures of his mother and Denise. The girl Keith had thought was perfect, as opposed to his daughter.

He told me you were too good for me.

Had he really told his own daughter that?

"What was your take on Keith McCauley?" Finn asked.

"Why do you ask?"

"Humor me," he said, dragging one hand over his face. "Give me your honest assessment of him."

"I know you thought the sun rose and set on the guy, and I liked him, too, but if you want the truth, I always thought he was kind of hard-nosed. A bit harsh. Wouldn't want to get on his wrong side."

Finn knew this, but hearing Vic say it in light of what Jodie had told him gave him another twist on things.

"Sorry, but you asked for my honest opinion," Vic continued. "There were times when I saw him lose it with the cows and was glad I wasn't the one he was mad at. Like I said, he helped you out a lot, and he helped me, too, but he had a hard edge, that's for sure."

As Vic spoke, Finn heard the truth in what he said, even as part of him fought it, feeling disloyal.

Had he been hero-worshipping the man? Had he been blind?

He used to hit me. Sometimes with an open hand. Sometimes with a fist.

"What's up?" Vic asked.

"I can't talk about it now. I'll tell you someday."

"And what about the horses?"

Finn scratched his forehead, trying to figure out what to do. "Just wait a day or two before you come and get them."

He hung up, then picked up his Bible. Right now he needed to set his feet on a solid foundation. What Vic had told him wasn't new, but combined with what Jodie had said, it altered his view of Keith.

Finn thought back to other things Jodie had said, before her revelation. How her father hadn't believed her when he'd picked her up at Jaden's party. How they used to have to sneak around when they were dating because she didn't want her dad to find out.

Finn had thought it was because she was ashamed of him, when it turned out she was probably afraid of Keith.

He suddenly recalled a model airplane he had put together once. His mother was away and he'd been by himself. He had gone ahead without the instructions, and when he saw it wasn't going the way it was supposed to, he'd started pushing pieces to fit, discarding the ones that didn't work.

Had he done the same with his relationship with Keith? Had he pushed things to fit, turning Keith into the father he had lost? Had that twisted his perceptions of the man, turning him into what was missing in his life?

Had he been blind to Keith's faults because he'd needed so badly for him to be good? So he could have someone to look up to?

Finn thought of what Vic had just said and knew

that Keith had a temper, and that he was only human. But he wanted so badly for Keith to be what he needed him to be.

He looked over at the pictures of Denise again and, with a smile, realized that even she was only human, and he couldn't compare her to Jodie. She hadn't lived the life Jodie had.

As he gazed at Denise, he knew he wasn't looking for someone like her anymore.

He was looking for someone like Jodie.

Chapter Seventeen

You should stay.

Jodie ignored the nagging voice as she carried her suitcase out to the car the next morning.

Stop running. Go talk to Finn. Explain.

Jodie's steps faltered as she thought of him. Explain what? she wondered, yanking open the door of her car. Give him the gory details? Would that make a difference? Would he believe her?

She tossed her suitcase onto the seat, then looked back at the house.

She'd left her father's letter behind, needing some space from it. Some distance while she tried to think what to do about it.

She sent up a prayer for strength and wisdom, then got into the car and drove away from the ranch.

At the end of the driveway she slowed. Right was the road back to Wichita. Left was the way to town, Saddlebank River and Finn's place.

She stopped there, her hands resting on the steering wheel. Turning to the right was running away.

Turning left meant facing her fears. Facing Finn.

"I'll need You beside me, Lord," she said aloud as she made her decision.

She had driven half a mile when she saw it.

A police cruiser.

She automatically slowed up.

Was it… Could it be…?

The cruiser flashed its lights, sped past her as she pulled over, turned around and parked behind her.

The driver got out, and as he walked toward her, Jodie felt as if her life had come full circle, back to where she had started only a few weeks ago.

But this time she didn't wait in the car, stifling her nervousness, hoping she wouldn't get dinged with a speeding ticket. This time she got out and stood by her vehicle, head up, facing Finn Hicks as he removed his sunglasses and tucked them in his pocket.

He didn't look as intimidating this time as he had the last.

She was surprised to see weariness in his expression and wariness in his eyes.

"Hey, Finn," she said. "I wasn't speeding this time."

"No. You weren't."

"So why did you stop me?" The question was meant to be teasing, but Jodie couldn't keep the yearning out of it.

"Because I don't want you to go." Finn took another tentative step toward her, raising his hand as if reaching out to her. "I want you to stay." He touched her shoulder, the faintest brush of his palm. "I'm sorry I didn't believe you. About your father. It was…difficult to hear…and unexpected. But I shouldn't have reacted the way I did."

Jodie was surprised at the tears that welled up in her eyes.

"I know your father was a hard man. I just didn't know how hard." Finn stopped there, his hand resting on her shoulder now, tightening. "I should have believed you. I'm sorry."

Sorry.

Had she ever heard that word from a man before?

Jodie's lips quivered, then she reached up and caught his hand in hers, holding it tightly. "Thank you," she whispered.

"Were you leaving?"

Jodie shook her head. "No. I was heading toward your place. To talk to you. I'm tired of running. I want to work this out."

"Me, too. Because I want good things for you, for us. I love you."

Joy swept through her soul like a spring Montana wind as she stared at him. "I love you, too," she choked out.

Then, to her surprise, he swept her into his arms and kissed her. She wove her arms around his neck, vaguely aware of knocking off his Stetson.

But then he kissed her again and she couldn't think of anything else.

Finally, he drew away, his rough finger tracing the tracks of her tears. "I'm sorry. I didn't mean to make you sad."

"I'm not sad. I'm happy. Happier than I've been in a long time."

Finn smiled and brushed a light kiss over her lips. "Me, too."

They stood this way for a moment, then Finn drew back. "I meant what I said," he told her. "When I said I was sorry that I didn't believe you. About your father. It was a shock for me."

"I shouldn't have run away," she admitted. "It was just so hard to see the look on your face when I told you. I just want you to believe me," she whispered, swiping at the tears on her cheek. "To know my side of the story. I'm sorry that it's not what you want to hear."

"You have nothing to be sorry about," he said, putting his knuckle under her chin and lifting her face to his. "I'm more upset for you than I am for any false vision I had of your dad. How he hurt you. How he took away your chance to go to that music school. Stole your future."

"It wasn't just him," she said, sniffing, wishing the tears would stop, thinking of the letters she had left in her father's house. "I made decisions, too. I could have tried again."

"But it changed everything for you."

"It did. But one of the biggest disappointments was missing out on whatever might have happened between us. If we had gone on that date, I think a lot would have changed. If I hadn't gone to that party, tried to defy my father one more time, everything could have changed, too. I made some bad choices back then."

"I'm sorry it seemed as though I didn't believe you," Finn responded. "It was just that I had such a different view of your father."

"I know that," she said. "I have to accept that the relationship you had with him was just a different side of who he was. I often wished I could have had the same relationship."

Finn gave her a soulful smile. "Your father helped me when I needed it. I felt I could trust him."

Jodie sensed the comfort he must have felt, being around her father and his never-ending rules.

"I wish you would have told me earlier about your dad," he continued. "I could have had time to readjust my thoughts. My expectations. My memories." He held her gaze, his own eyes tortured. "I always prided myself on knowing people, but in your dad's case I was wrong."

Jodie heard the pain in his voice at the loss of a part of his past. At the disillusionment he felt.

But her father's letters had given her a new perspective on an old relationship.

"'Stumbling to grace,'" she murmured.

Finn looked confused.

"Words from one of Mandie's songs," Jodie said. "I quoted them to you before. I think my dad was struggling, as well. Trying to do what he could, but not sure how. He wrote me a letter apologizing for what he did. It will take time for me to completely forgive him. For the memories of what he did to fade away."

She caught Finn's hands between hers. "We each had different relationships with the man," she said. "What happened between him and me was part of his identity, but it wasn't all of who he was. When I hear you talk about my father, truth be told, part of me is jealous. I wanted to have that, but I wasn't the perfect daughter."

A rueful smile drifted over Finn's dear features. "I can't believe you can be so gracious," he said.

She sighed, reaching out and stroking his face. "I know that all my mistakes have brought me here. To you." She cupped his cheek, the whiskers scratchy against her palm. "And I like where I am. Right now. Right here."

Finn closed his eyes, his hand covering hers as he

pressed a kiss to her palm. Then he held her gaze. "I am amazed at your capacity to forgive. Humbled by it, in fact. Now that I know what I do about your father, I feel as if I'm nowhere near ready to forgive him the way you have."

"Each of us has to find our own way to reconcile with people who have hurt us. Keith wasn't the best father, but I have to admit he did provide for us. I found that out."

"Just like I want to for my family," Finn said as he brushed a strand of hair from her face. "I think we were meant to be together, you and me. And I don't want you to ever leave. I want to marry you and provide for you and take care of you."

Jodie stared at him in wonder.

He kissed her again, as if sealing the promise, then drew back. "I want to be your husband, and I want to help you be the best person you can be. I want to help you nurture the gifts God has given you. I want you by my side as we grow old together."

Jodie flung her arms around his neck and kissed him again, her heart fuller than she'd ever thought it could be. "I love you, Finn Hicks. I think I always have. I want to stay here and be your wife."

"I've been wanting to tell you something all night," he told her. "I finally took your advice and bought the place I'm living. So I also have a home for us."

Jodie felt peace slip over her weary soul. "A home," she said, almost reverently. "I feel as though I haven't had that in a long time."

"You'll have one when we get married, and I want to do that as soon as possible."

Jodie kissed him again. "But I have to stay on the ranch…"

"Only another month."

"If I want my share," she said, a touch of remorse washing over her. "I'm not so sure I do. Part of me just wants to leave all that behind."

"It's your choice," Finn stated. "I can support us just fine without any money coming from your father's estate."

"I can pay my own way," Jodie said, teasing him now. "Mandie liked my music. Said she wanted to see more."

"I'm not surprised." Finn wove his fingers with hers.

"The piano," Jodie said suddenly. "I do want the piano from my father's place."

"I'm sure we can find a spot in the house for it." Finn smiled. "Just make sure you keep a place in your heart for me."

"You have all of my heart," she declared, giving him another kiss.

"I think we should celebrate. Lunch at the Grill and Chill? We can make some plans. For our future."

Love and peace and hope flowed through Jodie like a refreshing stream. "Lunch sounds good. And our future sounds even better." Then she gave him an impish grin. "Race you there?"

He laughed. "I don't think so. Then I'd have to give you a ticket."

"Like you should have the first time."

"I'm still glad I didn't. I needed all the points I could get with you."

Jodie's heart was so full she thought it would burst. Then he kissed her and touched her nose. "Don't speed," he warned her, before walking back to his cruiser.

Jodie watched him go, her smile so wide it hurt her face. Then she looked to the sky, which hung like a large blue bowl above her.

"Thank You, Lord," she whispered. "Thank You for bringing me back here. Back home."

Then she got into her car and followed her future husband to town.

And their new life together.

* * * * *

Keep reading for an exclusive excerpt of
THE RAIN SPARROW by
New York Times *bestselling author Linda Goodnight.*
Available now from HQN Books!

Dear Reader,

I think many of us struggle at one time or another with feeling we are not good enough. This is something Jodie had to deal with. Her father saw her as a burden and struggled with his feelings for her based on what he thought. This, of course, had a huge impact on Jodie and what she felt she was worth, and was reflected in the choices she made. But through the events of the story she learned her worth was not tied up in people's perceptions or what she thought others thought of her, but in how God saw her. If you are struggling with this same sense that you are not worthy, I pray that you may know that God sees you as infinitely precious. And that you are worth much to Him.

If you want to find out more about my books and stay on top of what's going on, sign up for my newsletter at www.carolyneaarsen.com or write to me at caarsen@xplornet.com.

Blessings,

Carolyne Aarsen

*A mystery writer and a shy librarian find love on a
dark, stormy night in Honey Ridge, Tennessee...*

BARE FEET SOUNDLESS on the cool tile flooring, Carrie
moved to a pantry and removed one of Julia's sterling
silver French press urns. "We'll have to grind the beans.
Julia's a bit of a coffee snob."

"Won't the noise disturb the others?"

Thunder rattled the house. Carrie tilted her head toward the dark, rain-drenched window. "Will it matter?"

"Point taken. You're a lifesaver. What's your name?"

"Carrie Riley." She kept her hands busy and her
eyes on the work. The fact that she was ever-so-slightly
aware of the stranger with the poet's face in a womanly
kind of way gave her a funny tingle. She seldom tin-
gled, and she didn't flirt. She was no good at that kind
of thing. Just ask her sisters. "Yours?"

"Hayden Winters."

"Nice to meet you, Hayden." She held up a canister
of coffee beans. "Bold?"

"I can be."

She laughed, shocked to think this handsome man might actually be flirting a little. Even if she wasn't. "Bold, it is."

As she'd predicted, the storm noise covered the grinding sound and in fewer than ten minutes, the silver pot's lever was pressed and the coffee was poured. The dark, bold aroma filled the kitchen, a pleasing warmth against the rain-induced chill.

Hayden Winters offered her the first cup, a courteous gesture that made her like him, and then sipped his. "You know your way around a bold roast."

"Former Starbucks barista who loves coffee."

"A kindred spirit. I live on the stuff, especially when I'm working, which I should be doing."

She didn't want him to leave. Not because he was hot—which he was—but because she didn't want to be alone in the storm, and no one else was up. "You work at night?"

"Stormy nights are my favorite."

Which, in her book, meant he was a little off-center. "What do you do?"

He studied her for a moment and, with his expression a peculiar mix of amusement and malevolence, said quietly, matter-of-factly, "I kill people."

COMING NEXT MONTH FROM
Love Inspired®

Available March 22, 2016

ELIJAH AND THE WIDOW
Lancaster County Weddings • by Rebecca Kertz

Hiring the Lapp family men to make repairs around her farmhouse, Martha King soon develops feelings for the younger Elijah Lapp. Now it's up to the handsome entrepreneur to show the lovely widow that age is no barrier for true love.

THE FIREFIGHTER DADDY • by Margaret Daley

Suddenly a dad to his two precocious nieces, firefighter Liam McGregory enlists hairdresser Sarah Blackburn for help. He's quickly head over heels for the caring beauty, but will the secret he keeps prevent them from becoming a family?

COMING HOME TO TEXAS
Blue Thorn Ranch • by Allie Pleiter

Returning to her childhood ranch, Ellie Buckton teams up with deputy sheriff Nash Larson to teach after-school classes to the town's troubled teens. Can she put her failed engagement in the past and find a future with the charming lawman?

HER SMALL-TOWN ROMANCE • by Jill Kemerer

Jade Emerson grew up believing Lake Endwell, Michigan, was a place where dreams come true. So why is Bryan Sheffield leaving? Can she convince the rugged bachelor to give his hometown—and love—a second chance?

FALLING FOR THE MILLIONAIRE
Village of Hope • by Merrillee Whren

When Hudson Conrick's construction company works on the women's shelter expansion at the Village of Hope, he'll prove to ministry director Melody Hammond that he's more than just an adventure-loving millionaire—he's her perfect match.

THE NANNY'S SECRET CHILD
Home to Dover • by Lorraine Beatty

Widower Gil Montgomery is clueless on how to connect with his adopted daughter—until he hires nanny Julie Bishop. He quickly notices she has a special way of reaching his little girl—and of claiming his heart.

LOOK FOR THESE AND OTHER LOVE INSPIRED BOOKS WHEREVER BOOKS ARE SOLD, INCLUDING MOST BOOKSTORES, SUPERMARKETS, DISCOUNT STORES AND DRUGSTORES.

LICNM0316

REQUEST YOUR FREE BOOKS!

2 FREE INSPIRATIONAL NOVELS
PLUS 2
FREE
MYSTERY GIFTS

Love Inspired®

LI15

EXCLUSIVE
Limited Time Offer

NEW YORK TIMES BESTSELLING AUTHOR
LINDA GOODNIGHT

THE
RAIN
SPARROW

A HONEY RIDGE NOVEL

$15.99 U.S./$18.99 CAN.

$1.50 OFF

New York Times Bestselling Author
LINDA GOODNIGHT
welcomes you back home to
Honey Ridge, Tennessee, with another
beautiful story full of hope, haunting
mystery and the power to win your heart.

THE
RAIN
SPARROW

Available February 23, 2016.
Pick up your copy today!

HQN™

$1.50 OFF
the purchase price of THE RAIN SPARROW
by Linda Goodnight.

Offer valid from February 23, 2016, to March 31, 2016.
Redeemable at participating retail outlets. Not redeemable at Barnes & Noble.
Limit one coupon per purchase. Valid in the U.S.A. and Canada only.

52613252

5 65373 00078 6 (8100)0 12117

PHLG0316COUP

Turn your love of reading into rewards you'll love with
Harlequin My Rewards

**Join for FREE today at
www.HarlequinMyRewards.com**

Earn **FREE BOOKS** of your choice.

Experience **EXCLUSIVE OFFERS** and contests.

Enjoy **BOOK RECOMMENDATIONS**
selected just for you.

PLUS! Sign up now
and get **500** points
right away!

Earn **FREE** REWARDS
Join Today!
HarlequinMyRewards.com

MYR16R